THE HOLIDAY REBOUND

EMILY BYBEE

5 PRINCE PUBLISHING

Published by 5 PRINCE PUBLISHING & BOOKS, LLC

PO Box 865, Arvada, CO 80001

www.5PrinceBooks.com

ISBN digital: 978-1-63112-350-4

ISBN print: 978-1-63112-352-8

Cover Credit: Marianne Nowicki

F10172023

*To my mom, one of the most
wonderful people in the world. Period.*

ACKNOWLEDGMENTS

Thank you first to my readers who support my stories and help me continue to write.

Second, thank you to my critique group who always calls me on my weak spots. Our group is so special and I am grateful for each one of you being in my life.

Next, thank you to Bernadette for encouraging me to get her this story and to Cate for helping clean it up and make it presentable to the world.

Lastly, thank you to my wonderful husband who put up with random weird questions like 'How many cranes would you have downtown to put up a couple high rises?' and so many more.

ALSO BY EMILY BYBEE

Merry Mix-Ups

The Holiday Rebound

THE HOLIDAY REBOUND

CHAPTER 1

REMI

"WHAT DO YOU MEAN YOU *ACCIDENTALLY* GOT HER PREGNANT?" I spat. "Like that makes it better?"

Mark held out both hands like a clueless zookeeper trying to calm a furious animal. "I love you, Remi. I had a slip up." He took a step toward me. "We can work this out."

I backed up as far as the countertop of the kitchen would allow. "Oh no. We're not working anything out." I gripped the ring on my finger and twisted. The metal cut into my skin as it ripped over my knuckle. I hadn't taken it off since the day Mark had proposed. I held out the circle of metal that had once signified unending love. "Why don't you give this to your slip up and ask her to marry you?"

"You don't mean that. I was drunk, and Kerri was there." He blocked my exit from the kitchen. Behind him, a little black muzzle and golden-brown eyes peered around at me, Mark's favorite work shoe in his mouth. The pup hunched over and let his head fall, obviously upset by our raised voices, and gnawed the leather in earnest.

Mark's words sunk in and I jerked my attention away

from the destructive puppy. "Wait, Kerri? As in Kerri, your assistant?"

His darting eyes gave him away before he spoke. "We were working late—"

I cut off his pathetic explanation. "As in the Kerri that I specifically asked if you were sleeping with?" I'd seen the way she looked at him. And the way he looked at her. It was hard to ignore when we all worked in the same office. But he'd patently denied anything between them, and being my stupid, trusting self, I'd believed him.

Anger bubbled up with the acid in my guts. I threw the ring at Mark as hard as I could. My aim was true, and the diamond bounced off his eyebrow, leaving a bloody cut, then clattered to the floor. I guess the gaudy two-point-five carat rock had some use besides showing Mark's ego. He'd made a point of telling everyone how much it had cost.

"Hey," Mark exclaimed and covered his eye with his hand. A dribble of blood traced down his face.

"How long has this been going on?" *Why didn't I trust my gut?*

"A while," he hedged.

"How long?" I ground out the words.

"Six months, maybe a little more."

The words doused any embers of love still hidden in my heart. *Right when I'd started to suspect something was up.* I pointed at the door. "Get out."

"Remi," he protested. "Just let me work this out."

"I said, get out." I picked up his favorite beer mug, a souvenir from our trip to Germany, and cocked my arm back. "Now."

He backed toward the door. "Okay, okay. I'll let you calm down a little and we can talk later." He paused in the doorway and flipped his blond hair in an oh-so-familiar move I used to find drool-worthy, but now it intensified my urge to break something over his head. "We were meant to be together. You'll see that."

The beer mug shattered against the door as it closed behind him. I hadn't even realized I'd thrown it. I stood and clung to the counter to stay upright as my world tilted. My brain couldn't process more than fragments of thoughts. Mark. Another woman. Not just any other woman, Kerri, who'd claimed to be my friend.

She's pregnant.

Had there been other affairs?

Then, an even worse thought increased the flood of upset.

My God, how am I going to face everyone at work? We worked in a small marketing firm. Everyone knew everyone. And the death of our relationship would be at the top of the office gossip.

I slid down the cupboards and crumpled to a puddle on the cold tile floor. With my palms pressed against my eyes, I refused to give in to the tears that wanted to pour out of me in a waterfall. Soft whimpers and a wet nose broke me from the darkness that surrounded me like a blanket.

"Hey, little man." I opened my eyes and picked up the fuzzy ball of black and brown fur that was intent on climbing me like a jungle gym. Warm slobber accompanied the tongue bath. "Gunner, no. Stop." I pushed his head down. He snuggled into my chest and rolled over to show me his round belly. At four months, the dog was still in the cute puppy stage. I rubbed his tummy and his head flopped to the side, his tongue lolling out.

The dog was Mark's—a present to himself disguised as worry over me being at home by myself at night—when he was working late, or rather, when he was getting Kerri pregnant.

Keeping a puppy with our work schedules hadn't been easy for the last two months. I got up to take the dog out in the middle of the night. I ran home on my lunch breaks to take him out. Our house didn't have a fenced-in yard, so walks and trips to the park took up much of my free time.

Now Mark would take Gunner when he came to get his stuff and I'd be truly alone. I hugged the puppy to my chest and let reality sink in.

"You broke up?" my mom gasped. "You were so happy. We paid the deposit to the caterer yesterday."

Though I'd tried to say the words, tried to tell her. I couldn't get the truth of the situation out. I leaned back in my chair and resisted the urge to pound my head against the table. Other patrons on the patio would probably notice. We were enjoying a break from the onset of the Colorado winter. A beautiful day in the sixties after snowstorms was one reason I swore I'd never move out of the state.

"I'm sorry, Mom. I would have called you, but I was in shock myself." After Mark's news, the last two weeks at work had been a nightmare, worse than that, absolute torture. I couldn't count the conversations that ended abruptly as I walked up, the pitying stares, the pats on my shoulder. Even my boss had asked if I needed to take time off.

I grabbed Gunner's leash before he made his way over to the table next to us, likely following the smell of a bacon burger. I pulled him back. Although he was only twenty pounds, he was getting stronger, and my muscles strained. "I'll pay you back for the deposit."

"You know that's not what I'm worried about," she said, and frowned. "Why do you have his dog?"

"It's important to socialize him. At least that's what the breeder said." I twisted as Gunner looped around the legs of my chair and tangled us both in the leash. "Besides, he was in his kennel too long yesterday while I was at work."

She reached across the table and put her hand on my arm. "You look terrible, honey. What aren't you telling me? Why did you break off the engagement?"

I hadn't told my mom about Mark *accidentally* getting someone pregnant for good reason. My brothers and dad might *accidentally* kill him, on my mom's orders. "He said he couldn't go through with the wedding." *Total lie.* "I was just as shocked as you." *That part's true at least.*

She set her credit card on the bill for lunch and brushed her perfectly styled hair away from her face. I adjusted the mess of a bun on top of my head and tucked a few strands that had escaped behind my ears as I wondered when I'd showered last—maybe my stench was the reason people were avoiding me at work? When had I fallen so low?

Gunner jumped up on my leg and tried to reach the French fries left on my plate. At least I didn't have to worry about the wedding diet anymore. I held out a fry to him and he gobbled it down in one bite, then licked his chops and waited for another, fully playing the I'm-a-cute-puppy card.

"You shouldn't feed him from the table." Mom shook her head. "Besides, the grease might upset his stomach."

The thought of Mark having to deal with puppy diarrhea made me hand over another French fry, or three. Gunner was thrilled.

"Now tell me exactly what happened with Mark," Mom insisted. "What were his exact words?"

I have something I have to tell you. I kinda got someone pregnant, accidentally. Those words had been playing on repeat inside my brain for the last week. *How do you* kind of *get someone pregnant?* "I don't remember, Mom." I grabbed my purse and unwrapped Gunner's leash from my chair. "And I have to go. Mark is picking up his stuff today and I have to give him Gunner."

The thought of having my only companion gone and being alone in the big house left me with mixed emotions. On one hand, sleeping in and not going for three walks a day sounded great. But tears pricked my eyes at the thought of handing over the unruly puppy. Pain in the butt that he was, he was so sweet.

"You're leaving? Do you want me to be there with you? I can call your dad or Jeremy."

"No," I gasped. The last thing I needed was for my brother to see the fallout and feel the need to step in as the protective older brother. "Sorry, I have to get back to the house." I stood.

"Isn't this all happening a little fast?" She grabbed her own purse as if to follow me, but had to wait on the bill. "You're together for three years and then in two weeks he's moving out?" Her face froze to marble. "Did he cheat?" Her jaw clenched. "I'm calling your brother."

"We can talk about it next time, Mom." I tried to run from the table and pulled Gunner, who'd decided to sit on the concrete behind me instead of following. "Sorry." *So not sorry.*

I made it back to the house and spotted Mark's truck out front and a rental truck in the driveway. Nausea threatened to bring the lunch back up for an encore performance. Besides at work, we'd spoken once in the two weeks since he'd broken the pregnancy news.

He'd wanted to let me know that he and Kerri had moved in together and were going to give the relationship a shot. Boy, was that a big turnaround from his claims that we were meant to be together.

The sound of his voice and the news they were now officially a couple had left me curled up in bed, this time in tears.

Gunner, hearing my distress, decided the best way to handle the situation was to grab mouthfuls of my hair and tug until I paid attention to him. Rubbing his soft fur had calmed me down a bit.

The next day Kerri had been waltzing around the office like a princess at a ball. *Was it bad to want to hit a pregnant woman? Definitely. No hitting.* But I'd brought in doughnuts every morning for the rest of the week—a particular weakness of Kerri's. Call me passive-aggressive. I needed some bit of joy in my life.

Mark and his best friend appeared from the side of the house, a TV balanced between them. My sad, sappy feelings mutated to anger in a second flat.

"Hey." I stormed over. "I bought the TV."

They paused, balancing the enormous TV on their legs. "As a Christmas present to me," Mark said.

"You'll be getting back all the presents you gave me, trust me." I barged inside and grabbed every present Mark had given me. It was easy considering they were all jewelry—diamond earrings, a matching tennis bracelet, an emerald necklace—my birthstone. I hated green. Every holiday, birthday, or major argument, I could count on a small box with a bow.

I stared at what our relationship amounted to, all in the palm of my hand. It was probably over thirty thousand dollars worth of jewelry. And I'd never wear a single piece again. I hadn't ever liked flashy jewelry to begin with, only wearing them to please Mark.

I stormed back out of the house and held out the fistful of diamonds and gems.

Mark blinked, having secured the TV to the side of the moving van while several other men carried various furniture that we'd picked out together. "Those were gifts for you. Keep them."

"You think I want anything you gave me?" I laughed. "Kerri would like them."

He held up his hands as the other guys moved away from our argument. "I know I hurt you, Remi." His voice was all soft and sincere. What a joke. "I'm truly sorry. I can put the TV back if it means that much to you."

Steel infused my spine. He didn't get to comfort me. He didn't get to make himself feel better. Like he was the bigger person in the situation. Lifting my chin, I stepped away. "Don't worry about it. I don't want anything. Take every damn piece of furniture in the house." I held out Gunner's leash. He sat by my feet and stared at Mark. A low puppy growl sounded in his throat. "He's had a walk today."

Mark eyed the dog like he was a piece of gum stuck to his shoe. "I can't take the puppy."

My gaze jerked back to his face that I once found so handsome but now reminded me more of a worm—actually, that insulted worms. "What?"

"Kerri doesn't like dogs." He shifted his weight. "So, you get to keep him."

My jaw dropped. No words formed. I glanced down at the fluff ball attached to my leg as my insides twisted into a knotted mess.

He nibbled on my jeans.

I'd said I'd miss him. But taking care of him was a full-time job.

"Or take him to the pound," Mark said. "Whatever makes you happy."

"The pound?" I spat and picked Gunner up, every protective instinct in my body on high alert. His warm muzzle nuzzled my neck. I had no idea how I'd manage taking care of the pup. But I'd figure it out.

❄

I SAT IN A NEARLY EMPTY HOUSE. THE JEWELRY THAT MARK had refused to take back lay on the coffee table, the single remaining piece of living room furniture. As I examined the seemingly random furniture that Mark had left, a pattern emerged—they all had chew marks on them from Gunner.

The pup lay on his back, absently gnawing on the single barstool that sat at the island counter. His teeth, sharp as a piranha's, shredded the wood with ease. I didn't have the energy to correct him or even care. I stared back down at the note I'd found after Mark left.

I'll have the real estate agent see about getting the house on the market.

Gunner barked and snagged the paper out of my hand, ripping it into shreds.

"I second that thought," I said and gave him a ruffle behind his ear. "And don't worry. No way am I taking you to the pound."

Gunner lifted his chin, his eyes solemn, as if he knew I was being serious. He licked my chin and lay across my chest with a contented sigh. "It's you and me, buddy."

CHAPTER 2

CADE

I GLANCED UP AT THE CASTLE-LIKE ROCK FROM MY BEDROOM window and a tight breath left my chest. The town namesake, the towering outcropping of rock, jutted up from north of old Main Street, Castle Rock.

It was like a lighthouse in a storm for sailors. It meant home. To think I'd let *her* chase me out of my hometown for almost three years. The job offer had been a great opportunity and now the supervisory project manager position graced the top of my resume—likely what had gotten me my new higher paying job back home in Colorado.

The northwest was beautiful, and I'd hiked some amazing waterfalls while living there, never really getting over how green everything was. But Colorado was home and after a couple of winters of not seeing the sun for weeks on end, I couldn't take it anymore. The three hundred plus days of sunshine per year beckoned me back.

I dropped the curtain and paced around the small bedroom. This happened every time I went out. Castle Rock wasn't a tiny town, and it was getting bigger by the day with people moving in. But it was small enough that you ran into people all the time. Eventually I'd run into *her*.

It shouldn't hurt so much. Who was I kidding? I hadn't even dated since she'd dumped me at the altar—literally—on Christmas day, no less. Sure, a few flings, but nothing remotely serious. That part of me died when Sara told me in no uncertain terms that she didn't love me anymore.

My phone buzzed and I answered. "Hey, Jeremy. What's up?"

"You coming out for beers tonight?"

"Ah," I hedged. "What about if we go up to Denver?"

"Man, come on." I could hear the eye roll. Being friends since grade school had its drawbacks. The main one being he knew me too well. "You can't avoid going out forever. You've been back for months and all we do is hang out watching football at my place."

"You've got a big TV." It wasn't really manly to admit that I still didn't think I could face my ex. Guys were supposed to shove those feelings down and act fine. Not something I'd ever excelled at.

"Just come out to the brewery on Wilcox. I'm sure Sara wouldn't show her face there."

I sighed. "Okay. I've got to run some errands, but then I'll meet you over there."

"Good to hear you're not cooped up in your apartment with the curtains drawn."

I glanced at the closed curtains. "Nope, got to get some stuff from the hardware store to fix this closet."

"See you later." Jeremy disconnected.

Straightening my back like I was preparing for way more than a trip to the hardware store, I headed out to my truck. Since I'd moved back, I'd avoided any place Sara might frequent, even shopped at off hours to avoid the chance of running into her at the grocery store. *This is ridiculous. If I see her, no big deal.*

My optimism lasted all the way to the big box store off I-25 and I actually felt half-way normal as I pushed my cart through the aisles until I came face to face with a twelve-foot Santa. Christmas blow-up decorations and light displays filled the front of the store. *It's barely November.* My teeth ground together. If I could skip the next two months, life would be a million times better. At least this year I wouldn't be alone on Christmas.

Pushing past the garish displays, I grabbed a tube of caulk, a new paintbrush, and some brackets for shelves. Barking turned my head as a puppy, a shepherd mix from the coloring, dragged a woman down the aisle by her wrist.

"Gunner. No," the woman said without enthusiasm or conviction. "Come."

Completely ignoring the commands, the pup dashed toward me. Without thinking, I stepped in front of the animal and held up a hand.

"Sit," I ordered, not leaving any room for interpretation.

Brown eyes met mine, and a furry butt hit the concrete with a thump. He stared up at me, as if waiting for his next instruction.

"How did you do that?" a vaguely familiar voice gasped.

I looked up as the woman pushed her long brown hair out of her face.

"Remi?" I asked and stared at my best friends' sister.

She blinked, then really looked at me. "Cade?"

The pup picked up on the excitement in her voice and his whapping tail merged into a full-on butt wiggle. He was about to break. "Stay," I ordered.

He calmed immediately and I returned my attention to Remi. She'd changed in the last few years. There was no sign of the kid I'd grown up with. Instead, stood a beautiful woman, hair to her waist and a touch of sadness around her tired green eyes.

She flashed a genuine smile and there was the Remi I'd known.

"Jeremy said you were back." Being about a foot shorter than me, she reached to wrap me in a hug. "I'm sorry I haven't been around. This one has been keeping me busy." She motioned to the dog when she released me. "How did you get him to listen?"

"You need to mean what you say." I cocked my head to the side and considered the shadows under her eyes. She appeared tired, and not just from lack of sleep. "You doing okay?"

Her eyes glistened with moisture, but she threw on another smile and waved me off. "I'm great. Tons going on at work and getting lots of exercise because he needs like three walks a day."

I wasn't buying it. I'd have to ask Jeremy what was going on when I saw him.

"How are you doing?" she asked. "I haven't seen you since the day after…"

She stopped herself before she said the wedding.

"…since Christmas three years ago. We missed having you at the house the last couple years," she recovered. "Will you be over this year?"

"Wouldn't miss it." Genuine warmth enveloped me at the memories of so many years of holidays spent with Remi and Jeremy's family. Someone knocking into me from behind evaporated the warmth like mist.

I turned, an apology already on my lips, and my muscles froze. I stared gape-mouthed at my worst nightmare in the flesh. Sara.

"Oh, excuse me," she said without looking up.

In a second flat, I took in the changes from the last couple years. She'd cut her blonde hair from mid-back to chin length and her make-up—always having to be perfect before—was now minimal. She glanced up and her expression mirrored mine as recognition set in.

"Cade," she gasped. "I didn't know you were back in town."

I snapped my mouth shut, moving about as far away as I could manage in the aisle, and stepped closer to Remi. "Got back a few months ago."

A forced smile graced her lips. "Well, I'm so glad you're back in Colorado."

I didn't believe that for a second. But I nodded and wondered how long you were expected to stand and talk to an ex that left you at the altar. One minute? Two? How long to prove you were over them? And I really needed her to believe that I was over her.

Her gaze rested on Remi, and she smiled. "We've met before."

"At the wedding," Remi said without mincing words. "Right before you made your speech and left."

Sara's face hardened, and her smile fell.

God. That speech. In front of everyone. Detailing why she didn't love me and couldn't marry me. My skin pricked with sweat. Was it hot in here? I unzipped my jacket. The pup, forgotten at my feet for too long, broke and wrapped the leash around my legs as he explored the many toxic substances he was considering chewing on.

I took the leash from Remi's hand and tugged up to get his attention. "Sit," I said again, thankful to look away from Sara. He thumped down and waited. "Good sit."

Sara's gaze darted between Remi and me. "I didn't realize you two had gotten together."

Without a second thought, my arm wrapped around Remi and pulled her to my side like she was my anchor in a hurricane. "Why else would I come back here?" I heard the words leave my mouth.

Remi glanced up at me, stiff at first, eyes wide, then her body softened against mine in a way that loosened some of the mess of knots inside me, and she winked. "Quit being so modest. You couldn't turn down the job." She put a hand on my chest as if we'd been together for years. "They offered him an obscene raise to poach him from his last company."

Remi obviously remembered the details of Sara's wedding speech as well. She'd said she needed to be with someone who could provide for her the way she wanted to live—and any construction job would never pay well enough. I'd seen that she'd moved in with a lawyer when I was totally *not* stalking her on Facebook in the lonely year after the wedding.

Sara chewed on her lower lip. "What are you doing now?"

"Same thing," I said, and let my hand run up and down Remi's arm. "But I'm a field supervisor now."

"Geez, too modest again," Remi laughed. "You know the four cranes down off I-25 and 225?"

Sara nodded. The enormous job site was hard to miss with the four high-rises going in.

"He's in charge of the entire job." Remi lifted her gaze back to mine and I spotted a familiar devilishness.

How did she know that was my job? Again, without thinking, I leaned down and kissed her forehead—surprising even myself. I didn't miss the tremor that shot through Remi. *Don't push your luck.*

"Well, good to see you, Sara," I said. "We should get this little man out of here." I motioned to the dog.

"Oh," Sara gasped, and dug into her purse. "You'll of course have to come to the holiday party. Everyone will want to see you…both." She handed me a rectangle of crisp press-board tastefully decorated in holiday colors.

"Oh, I'm not sure we can make it." I glanced at Remi.

"Wouldn't miss it," Remi said with enthusiasm that made me give her a second look.

She's really putting on a good show.

CHAPTER 3

REMI

I OPENED THE DOOR TO THE HOUSE AND WAVED CADE IN behind me. He'd refused to let me try to shove all the materials I was buying at the hardware store into my car and instead followed me home in his truck. I unhooked Gunner's leash and let him run free, already having let him potty in the front yard.

Glancing around the nearly empty rooms, I winced. I hadn't let anyone in since Mark moved out. "If you want to set the stuff down there, I can take it from here."

With a crusty glare at the Christmas decorations, he placed the box of the reindeer lawn ornaments that I'd bought, then set several large bags down on the floor where I'd indicated. His gaze moved over the bare room. I hadn't bothered to replace any of the furniture that Mark took besides the couch.

"Just move in?" he asked.

"No." I didn't meet his eyes. "Just got rid of some dead weight." I fidgeted with my bare ring finger.

"Jeremy said you were engaged." He walked into the kitchen. "Did he even leave you a spoon?"

"Two," I quipped and I followed him. "And a few cups. But he took most everything else." I'd at least replaced the kitchen essentials.

Cade shook his head. "What a peach. Where can I find him?"

I rolled my eyes, hard. "Don't you start. I have to work with the bastard. The last thing I need is him getting roughed up and me losing my job." I took two glasses from my new set in the cupboard and filled them with water and handed one to Cade. "So that was crazy running into Sara."

"Thanks for playing along. But I'm not expecting you to actually go to the party or anything." He took a long drink.

I straightened. "Are you kidding? I'm not letting you off that easy." The minute he'd put his arm around me and went along with Sara's misconception of us being a couple, a plan had formed in my mind. One that benefitted both of us. "We're going to that party."

He eyed me like a wild animal. What was it with guys giving me looks like that lately? Maybe I was a bit crazy. Maybe I really didn't care anymore.

"Why would we do that?" he choked out.

"How many Christmas and New Year's parties are you going to in the next two months that she might be at?" I asked.

He set his glass on the counter. "I'm not going to any. I hate Christmas."

"Come on. You're going to stay home and hide? Let her win? Like when she chased you out of town?" His face hardened and for a second I worried that I'd pushed too far. I softened my voice. "You should be out seeing friends that you haven't seen in years without worrying that you'll run into that bitch."

"Why do you care so much if I go to parties?" he asked.

I rounded the island and cocked my head to the side.

"Because I care about you." I waited a beat. "And I might need your help as well."

The no that had been forming on his lips died there. "With your ex?"

Refusing to let myself cry, I blinked and nodded. "I have to see him at the company party, not to mention two others that mutual friends are throwing." I gripped his forearm. "We can help each other get through all of it." He opened his mouth, but I rushed on. "You'd be doing me a huge favor and we'd have fun. We always had fun together."

He put his hands on my shoulder to stop my tirade. "Okay, Remi. Okay. You have me convinced."

"Really?" I'd never thought he'd really go for it. But the thought of missing all the things that I loved about the next two months had been driving me crazy for weeks. No way I could show my face all alone at those parties and watch Mark and Kerri all over each other.

But I could with Cade by my side.

"I don't care as much about missing the parties, but I have to admit that I liked the surprise on Sara's face." He grinned at the memory.

I hoped I could measure up to the tall blonde. "I promise to look extra hot to make her jealous."

He scoffed. "Like you have to try." He shook his head, his attention out the back windows to the unfenced yard.

I bit my lip as heat flooded my cheeks. His nonchalance at the statement tickled my stomach. Sara was model beautiful by any standards. My shorter, curvier build was more a matter of preference.

A grating sound broke me from my thoughts. "Gunner," I called. A fuzzy head poked around the corner, the wooden leg of the barstool in his mouth. "No, naughty puppy. Drop it."

He wagged his tail and trotted out, the entire barstool, which was twice his size, dragging behind him on the floor.

"I said drop it," I repeated.

Gunner sat on his haunches and chewed the wood in earnest while he gazed innocently at me with his huge puppy eyes.

"Drop it." Cade's voice echoed through the empty space and off the vaulted ceilings.

Gunner took his mouth off the leg and stared at Cade like he was a soldier and Cade was his superior officer.

I blew out a breath. "How do you do that?"

Cade walked over to where Gunner sat, as if waiting for him. "Good drop." He took the barstool and set it in front of the countertop. It now leaned toward the one side with the shorter, chewed leg. "You sound like you're asking him. Not telling him."

I crossed my arms. "I've had dogs before. I know how to train them. He doesn't listen."

"You've obviously taught him commands. He knows the meaning." Cade ruffled Gunner's head. "He doesn't think he has to listen to you. What kind of dog is he?"

I closed my eyes and rolled them. How I'd argued against getting such a high need dog. "Half German Shepherd and half Belgian Malinois. Mark bought him."

"Malinois?" Cade asked. "Geez. No wonder he knows all the commands." He spoke to Gunner. "You're a smart boy, aren't you? But you need a lot of structure."

"I work with him and walk him three times a day since he can't run outside." I motioned to the unfenced yard. "But he seems to be getting more unruly."

"I didn't say you weren't trying." Cade's attention settled on the roll of chain link in his truck bed. "You're going to build an enclosure for him out of that?"

I nodded.

"I'll be back in a bit." He started for the door.

"Where are you going?" I called. "We need to plan out the party schedule."

"Back to the hardware store. You're going to need an actual wooden fence."

WATCHING CADE IN A T-SHIRT, EVEN IN THE CHILLY November weather, was more distracting than it should have been. I'd known the guy nearly my entire life. He was practically a brother. The thought sent gross feelings racing up my spine. Okay, maybe not like a brother.

The sensation of his lips pressed against my forehead when he kissed me flashed in my mind. That had brought up some feelings as well. But the total opposite of gross.

He was out in my backyard, building me a fence—like around the entire backyard. I shook my head and watched him measure out where the posts needed to go. Another man had come with some equipment to do locates before Cade had dug with the auger—a huge corkscrew type machine that dug holes. Man, did that look like a workout.

He'd handed the man some cash for coming out on a Saturday at such short notice. *Nice thing about having friends in the trades.*

I slipped my jacket on and grabbed a bottle of water out of the fridge and Gunner's leash, then clipped him on. When Cade turned at the sound of the door opening, a smile cracked his serious expression. He took the water. "Thanks."

Gunner sniffed the fresh dirt and immediately began digging, sending dirt flying everywhere.

Cade shook his head.

"Should I tell him to stop?" I asked, not enjoying being so unsure of myself. But it was a feeling that seemed to permeate my bones the last month. Ever since I'd found out about the affair and the baby.

"Do you want him digging in your yard all the time?" Cade asked evenly.

Good way to look at it. I tried to put force behind my voice. "Gunner, leave it."

The pup completely ignored me, and his paws continued to fly through the earth.

Cade took the leash, gave it a sharp tug, and spoke, not loudly but firmly. "Leave it."

The dog stopped and sat down.

I threw my hands up in the air. "Geez. You should take him. He likes you better."

"Has nothing to do with who he likes, and you know it." Cade laid one arm over my shoulder in a comforting gesture.

I scrunched my mouth. "I've trained dogs before," I repeated. "Just never one this stubborn."

"Well, he needs a job. He's a working dog."

"Can he learn to do dishes?" I took the leash and walked Gunner over to where I'd taught him to do his business. "Go potty."

He leaned forward and peed.

"See," Cade said. "He listens to you."

I rolled my eyes for about the hundredth time. "So, when are the parties that you are invited to?"

He rested on the shovel that he'd been using to clean out loosened dirt from a hole. "You sure you want to do this? Do you think anyone will even believe we're a couple?"

"I'm sure." I walked back and leaned into him. My shoulder fit perfectly to the space on his ribcage and my head rested neatly against his chest. I considered his surprised eyes and nearly purred. "I think we can be plenty convincing."

I might have been crazy, but I swore something sparked in his eyes. Yeah, this was Cade we were talking about. I was probably crazy.

CHAPTER 4

CADE

I left Remi's house when the sun fell too low over the horizon to see. Her enthusiasm over this crazy charade that I'd accidentally started surprised me. But it really shouldn't. Remi had always been so sweet and outgoing, willing to do anything to make even a stranger happy. Was it really so surprising that she'd play along to help me?

The feel of her leaning against my chest flooded my senses, along with the smell of her hair when I'd kissed her on the forehead—clean with a light floral tone. *Holy shit. I kissed her. Not just any her, Remi.*

My stomach clenched with a sudden and extremely painful force.

Jeremy was going to kill me. How could I have not thought about this before? We couldn't possibly go through with this farce. Not unless I wanted to lose my best friend and end up beat bloody.

Stopped at a red light, I shot a text to Remi.

> Maybe we need to rethink this dating thing?

Her response was immediate.

> Don't you try to get out of this. I already
> RSVPd to the company party with a plus one.

There was a pause and dots showing she was texting again.

> Please don't make me try to find a date.

Remi could crook a finger and have five guys lining up to take her to this stupid party, and I started texting back. A horn from the car sitting behind me jerked my attention to the road and my phone dropped between the seats. Swearing, I drove the rest of the way to the brewery on Wilcox Street and spotted Jeremy's truck by the curb.

Retrieving my phone from the floorboard, I saw three more texts from Remi.

> Cade?

> Don't make me sic Gunner on you.

> Please?

THE LAST ONE GOT ME. HER SAD AND TIRED EYES FLASHED through my mind. There was definitely something more going on with this ex of hers. I knew all too well the pain of a broken heart. My shoulders tightened at the thought of telling Jeremy about the setup. How do you tell your best friend that you're fake dating their sister?

I swallowed and went inside, ready to face the music.

"There he is," Jeremy called from a booth and waved me over. "Thought you got lost."

I took the seat across from Jeremy. "I actually ran into Remi at the hardware store."

His brows lifted. "Really? What was she doing there?"

"Getting dragged around by a dog, actually." I grinned at the memory. "What happened with her and her ex? She seems off."

Jeremy grimaced and he white knuckled his beer mug. "I swear if I run into Mark..." He shook his head. "She says it was a mutual break up, but I've never seen her like this. She's hiding something."

I nodded and ordered a local brew when the waiter approached, considering. "They were together for a while, right?"

"Three years."

We sat for a minute in silence, then the waiter brought my beer. I sipped the IPA, smooth with a perfect bitter finish. "It was pretty low of him to take all the furniture from the house."

I didn't realize my mistake until Jeremy's assessing expression settled on me. I hadn't mentioned going to her house. Swallowing, I rushed to fix my mistake. "I helped her get some fencing back to the house with my truck."

Jeremy nodded, accepting my explanation without question. "She hasn't let any of the family inside."

"It wasn't a big deal. I carried stuff in for her." I shrugged. "And I helped with the dog."

"We know from Mitch, the real estate agent, that Mark wants to sell the house, but Remi is trying to keep it. She'll have to buy him out, which will be over eighty grand, and he's not budging on the timeline, bastard." Jeremy downed his beer and waved to the waiter for another. "Mom suspects he was cheating, but Remi won't talk about it." He leaned an arm over the back of the booth. "Will you do me a favor?"

"Anytime," I answered without pause.

"She seems to be more open to talking to you about this," Jeremy said, a gleam in his expression. "Keep an eye on her and let me know how badly I need to mess up Mark."

Sipping my beer, I nodded. "You going to beat him in an alley?" I was only half kidding. Jeremy had always been protective of his sister. "We're not in high school anymore."

"Nah, I've got way worse ways to get to him."

The expression on his face made me bite back the confession about the deal I'd made with Remi. I had absolutely no idea how Jeremy would react to the situation. *Now isn't the time to bring that up. Don't want to ruin the night.*

Jeremy waved as two guys came in the door, rescuing me from more conversation about Remi and feeling like I was keeping something from my best friend—which I was.

SUNDAY, I WENT BACK TO REMI'S EARLY TO GET WORKING ON the fence. Knowing that she was trying to buy Mark out of the house, there was no way I was going to take her money for the lumber. She had bigger things to worry about.

Remi's bleary-eyed face poked out of the back slider and Gunner dashed out, running to my feet and sniffing the fresh dirt. The fuzz ball, still covered with a good amount of the ultra-soft puppy fur, dropped and rolled in the moist earth.

"Great," Remi sighed as the pup reveled in the dirt. He looked up at her and sneezed, his tongue lolling out to one side with a contented expression. "Now you need a bath."

He sniffed out a rock, sneezing again, and scraped his teeth along it. I dug the rock out of his mouth, tossed it to the other side of the yard, and replaced it with a stick. "Here, chew on this."

He watched where I threw the rock but munched the stick.

"It's like he's a piranha, but with fur." Remi crossed her arms. "I love him, but he's a lot of work."

I nodded. "He's not the easiest breed. That's for sure."

"What can I do to help with the fence?" She motioned to the piles of pickets and cross beams.

"You don't have to help." I shook my head. "I got this."

She picked up a cross beam, slipping Gunner's leash around her ankle. "No way. I'm not letting you do all the work."

I knew better than to argue with her when she had that determined expression on her face. Last time I'd tried to talk her out of something, she drank a twelve pack of beers at a high school party, just to prove me wrong when I'd said she should stop, and I ended up carrying her to the car to drive her home.

Several hours later, we'd made good progress, finishing two sides of the yard, and getting ready to start on the third. We worked in concert, easily and with little talk.

"Hand me that impact?" I asked, pointing to the tool by her feet.

Remi leaned to pass the tool over.

Gunner, spotting a rabbit, sprang to his feet and dashed after the gray bunny. His leash jerked taut and yanked him to a stop but not before wrenching Remi's foot out from under her. Her eyes widened and she tumbled headlong toward the freshly built section of fence.

Without a thought, I lunged to catch her. We ended up in a pile on the dormant grass, Remi on top of me, held tight in my arms. Her chest pressed against mine.

She lifted her head. "Are you okay?"

I stared at her face, so close to mine. Her fresh and light floral scent washed over me. "I'm... I'm good." I sputtered. "You okay?"

Before she could answer, Gunner joined the pile, his cold nose and wet tongue seemingly everywhere as he wiggled between us, obviously thinking this was the greatest game ever. His flying tail smacked my face repeatedly and I tasted dirt and hair.

"Gunner," Remi laughed, trying and failing to push the puppy away. He licked and got his tongue in her mouth. She sputtered, then rolled off me. "Oh, gross. Gunner!"

I wiped my mouth on my sleeve and pushed up before the exuberant pup could tag me with his deadly tail or tongue again. Chuckling, I stood and offered Remi a hand.

Accepting, she brushed dead grass off her pants and spit. "Love puppy breath."

Gunner ran in circles, entwining our legs in his leash.

"I'll take him in for some water," Remi said. "And to brush my teeth."

As she walked toward the back door, he pulled to one side, another destination obviously in mind. Remi gave him some slack and he darted directly to the spot I'd thrown the rock hours earlier, plucking it from the grass and trotting happily after Remi.

I shook my head. *Damn smart pup.*

CHAPTER 5

REMI

I WALKED IN THE DOOR, DROPPED MY COMPUTER BAG AND purse on the floor, then collapsed on the couch—or what was left of it. The last two weeks of work had been from hell. No, that was putting it mildly. Hell would have been a vacation.

The only bright spots had been the days I saw Cade. He came over several times, even after we finished the fence, to help me train Gunner—not that it helped. At least Cade made me laugh and forget my pathetic life for a while.

Kerri had announced that she was pregnant to everyone at work. Just when things had been dying down in the rumor mill, she stirred it up again. So, I'd dealt with a fresh wave of sympathy, whispered conversations, and pats on the back until I'd wanted to scream.

I'd responded by making a special trip to every great doughnut shop in a twenty-mile radius to bring in treats. Every time Kerri snuck into the break room to grab *just one more,* my evil heart warmed. I'd heard her whispering that she'd already put on fifteen pounds, and what some might consider a sick wave of glee washed over me. I should have felt guilt, but I couldn't seem to summon the emotion.

As if that wasn't enough, our boss announced he was relocating to the main office in New York. He'd choose his replacement from our current team leads. Basically, either Mark would become my boss, or I'd become his. Most of the office figured Mark would get the promotion since he had two years of experience on me. I might be hunting for a new job. Working in the same office was one thing. No way could I handle taking orders from him.

Gunner jumped up and snuggled against my side.

"How did you get out?" I put my hands under his muzzle and looked into his sweet eyes. On top of everything, Gunner figured out how to open his kennel. I'd come home the last three days to him joyfully sitting in a fresh pile of feathers and ripped cushions from my new couch, happy as a pig in mud. I had no idea how he kept getting out of the kennel, but after being extra sure it was secure when I left and coming home to him free, I'd decided I needed to pick up a padlock.

He licked my chin, then leapt off me to go jingle the Christmas bells I'd hung from the back door—his way of telling me he needed to go outside. At least he never had accidents, which was amazing for a pup his age.

Forcing myself off the couch, I took him outside and shivered in the wintery wind. Next week was Thanksgiving. At least it was a short week at work. I glanced at the house. Mark and I had planned to host for our families in our new house. What a nightmare. I'd been hesitant about buying a house together before we were married, but he'd convinced me with prices rising and interest rates shooting up. Now I was stuck with a decision: sell and move, or buy him out, which would cost me three times the money that I'd put away in my savings.

The fresh scent of cedar washed over me and I considered the fence that Cade and I built. It surrounded the entire yard and gave Gunner room to run free. The fence was also the first project that I'd done on the house. When we'd bought it, Mark and I had talked about at least ten things we wanted to change. But when it came down to working on tile, or a new banister, it turned out he'd rather watch football.

That fence looks damn good. A sense of pride filled me along with a renewed determination to keep the place. I loved the neighborhood and the home, especially with my ideas of how to fix it up. I'd strung Christmas lights on the top of the fence and they switched on, casting a rainbow of colors in the fading evening light.

Gunner finished up and raced laps around the yard, seeming excited by the lights turning on.

"You goofy boy." I laughed as he raced by and dropped a ball at my feet. I threw it for him and he dashed across the dry grass. My phone dinged in my pocket. Cade texted.

> Pick you up at 7? Unless you've changed your mind…

Shit! The first party was tonight. This was one of Mark's and mine's mutual friends.

> Not a chance. See you soon.

I tossed the ball one more time for Gunner and mentally flipped through my wardrobe. Looking good wouldn't cut it. I needed to look *sexy-elf* hot.

THE BELL RANG AT SEVEN SHARP. I BRUSHED ONE LAST COAT OF mascara over my lashes, contemplating my reflection. *It's as good as it's going to get.*

I adjusted my strapless bra before I opened the door. Cade stood on the porch and Gunner rushed out to meet him. While he greeted the pup with enthusiastic pets, I took in a cleaned-up Cade. And took him in some more. I'd seen him in a dress shirt and slacks many times, even in a tux. But he was especially handsome tonight.

Tender wings of butterflies uncurled in my stomach and tickled my insides. I blinked at my reaction to the handsome man on my doorstep. But I'd known him nearly my whole life. And he'd always just been Cade.

I'm just happy he'll make Mark jealous. The thought didn't quite ring true even in my mind, but I brushed away the feeling.

"Ready to go drink eggnog and..." Cade's voice fell away as his gaze settled on me.

I smoothed my hands over the sequined dress and tugged at the short hem. I'd bought it on a whim a couple years ago, but never had the nerve to wear the mini-dress. Not only did it show a lot of leg, I wasn't used to displaying quite so much cleavage. "Is it too much? Maybe I should change."

Cade blinked as Gunner took his cuff in his front teeth and tugged. "No!" Cade exclaimed. "I mean, you look amazing." He pushed Gunner away, leaving two small holes in his sleeve from the puppy's teeth.

"You're sure?" I asked. "I don't want to embarrass myself. Just show up Mark a bit."

"You're missing one thing." He grabbed a Santa hat I'd tossed on the entryway table and settled it on my head, off to one side. "Now you're perfect."

"Sorry about your shirt." I motioned to the small holes in the crisp fabric and walked to the kitchen to throw a treat in the kennel. "He's started nibbling on my clothes whenever I get home."

Cade considered Gunner as he bounded into the kennel

and gobbled the treat. "Don't worry about the shirt. But we're going to have to break that habit. You ready to see Mark?"

I'd thought I was ready—even baking cookies to bring the host and buying a good bottle of wine. Now that the night was here, I wasn't so sure. I swallowed bile and pasted a smile on my lips. "Let's do this."

THE GLARE OF THE CHRISTMAS DECORATIONS GUIDED US TO the house from a block away.

Cade parked the car. "Looks like a reindeer barfed on a clearance sale at a blow-up factory."

Blow-up characters covered every inch of the yard, and a good portion of the roof. Plus, lights galore were strung along the length of the house.

I loved every gaudy holiday-inspired inch of it. "It's not that bad."

He huffed.

"Don't be a grinch," I said as we walked to the front door and waited. This party was more like a minefield. Mark had been a groomsman at the host's wedding while I'd been the Maid of Honor. And I'd caught the bouquet. That was how we'd met. Everything had seemed to fit so perfectly. Taking Cade's hand in mine, I shoved the memory away.

Sasha, my friend from high school, opened the door and let out a squeal. "You came!"

I held out the wine topped with a bow, still holding a plate of cookies. "Happy holidays!"

"Thank you!" She took the bottle and waved us inside with a crinkled brow as she studied Cade. "I recognize you."

"Sorry," I apologized. "You remember Cade? He was a couple of years ahead of us in school."

Her eyes widened. "That's right." She closed the door and sent me an OMG stare behind Cade's back while she fanned her face. "I was worried you wouldn't come."

"You know how much Remi loves a good holiday party," Cade put in, his gaze wandering over the five Christmas trees around the living room and the garland around the banister. "But I'm guessing you love the holidays as well."

"Guilty," Sasha said with a giggle that told me she'd started drinking early. "Mingle, there's plenty of food and drinks. You can put the cookies on the table in the dining room." She leaned to whisper in my ear. "And Mark showed up."

I nodded. Of course he did. He wouldn't miss a party. I pulled Cade through the crush of bodies. *Jingle Bell Rock* played over the din of voices. I waved to people I hadn't seen in months, smiled, and maybe clung to Cade's arm.

See, this won't be so bad.

We found the table loaded with enough food to feed an army.

And Kerri.

That didn't take long. She was loading up a plate with cookies and candy. Guess this pregnancy was giving her a sweet tooth for more than doughnuts.

I froze. Her dress was a loose fitting sleeveless that hung loose enough to hide her emerging baby bump. Guess she wasn't ready to tell everyone.

"What's wrong?" Cade asked so only I could hear.

I shook my head, then cleared my throat. "Nothing." I shoved the plate on the table without bothering to make room and turned away. "Are you thirsty?" I tried for chipper, but my voice sounded as squeaky as an elf huffing helium.

His frown told me I wasn't pulling off the cheerful vibe I was going for. "Whatever you want."

I spun, ignoring Kerri's wave of hello. *Freaking really? She has nerve. I'll give her that.*

Two steps toward the kitchen and I stopped. Mark filled the space. The smile faded from his lips when his gaze settled on me, and my skin heated as he took in my short dress, his gaze moving slowly down my body from head to toe.

"Remi," Mark said. "Hey, good to see you." His gaze hovered over my chest.

"Um, yeah, I brought cookies." *I brought cookies? What am I? Five? Way to sound like a moron.* I thought I wanted to get Mark's attention, to show him what he'd let go, but now I felt naked.

Cade stepped from behind me, angling his body and wrapping his arm around my waist in a possessive gesture that broke Mark's ogling of my cleavage. Cade didn't smile. He didn't offer his hand. He glared at Mark.

Kerri appeared beside Mark and plastered herself to his side like a barnacle. "We didn't think you'd come, Remi."

More like you were hoping I wouldn't.

Cade spoke up. "And you are?"

"Kerri," she bubbled. "Mark's girlfriend."

Cade's grip on me tightened and he straightened to his full height.

The tension in the room seemed palpable. How was everyone else still chatting, singing, dancing? I wanted to fall through the floor. I should have warned Cade about Kerri. Now he'd know Mark cheated.

"We were getting some drinks if you'll excuse us?" Cade said in a tone that barely scraped by as polite.

Mark stepped to block our exit. "Who are you, again?"

Cade leaned in, towering a good head over Mark, and practically growled. "Someone you don't want to know."

I barely heard the words, but the tone sent goosebumps erupting over my skin. Mark glowered, but stepped away.

"Come on, babe," Cade said and led me toward the kitchen. "Let's have some fun."

Out of Mark's sight, I slumped. This was harder than I'd thought. What was the point of coming to a party if it was pure torture? This whole idea was ridiculous, moronic, and stupid. "We should leave."

Cade gave me a squeeze, then released me to pour a glass of wine and grab a beer from the containers of drinks. "And waste that dress? We're going to dance."

"I'm not sure if I'm up for dancing." Inside, I felt weak, broken. Seeing Kerri and Mark at work was hard enough, but I wore my mask of indifference. This was a completely different story. "What's the point?" I whispered. "I want to go home."

Cade took my hand in his powerful grip and leaned down until I had to meet his gaze. "We always have fun together, remember?"

Half a smile crept over my lips. He pressed the wine into my hands, and I swallowed most of the glass. "Okay."

He led me to the dance floor. Thankfully, *I Gotta Feeling* was playing now instead of a Christmas song, and Cade wrapped his free arm around me, pulling me in close to his body and moving to the beat. The feel of his warm body pressed against mine let me take a breath. I knew he'd catch me if I fell. He had me.

And we always did have fun together.

We danced through the rest of the song, and the next, an upbeat jam that had Cade headbanging to make me laugh. Then, *Shake it Off* came on.

"I love this song," I shouted. The living room turned dance floor was getting crowded. Stepping back from Cade, I gave my shoulders a shake and lifted a brow at him.

Grinning widely, he took my hips in his large hands and matched my movements. He'd always been an excellent dancer, but I'd only ever been an observer. Couples gave us room and he spun me, then caught me easily, leading me from side to side, and as the song ended, he spun me out one more time, then snapped back to his chest.

Everyone clapped and I pressed my face to his shirt to catch my breath. Cade waved off the applause as a slow song started. I wrapped my arms around his neck and we swayed together.

"See," he whispered. "Aren't you glad you didn't leave?"

I sighed, a warmth filling my chest that I hadn't experienced in a long time.

"Look over to your left," Cade whispered.

I opened my eyes and caught sight of Mark watching us with a most peculiar expression on his face—definitely not cheerful.

"Does that make you happy?" Cade asked.

To my surprise, it didn't. I closed my eyes again and settled my head back on Cade's chest. So comfortable, so safe. I couldn't say the words that ran through my mind. They surprised me too much. *But you make me happy.*

CHAPTER 6

CADE

I HADN'T PRESSED REMI ABOUT THE OBVIOUS—MARK CHEATED on her. If she'd wanted to tell me, she would have. Controlling my anger and not punching the guy out had taken all the restraint I possessed—especially with him staring at her chest like he still had a right. We stayed at the party and I put everything I had into making sure that she had fun, even playing the ridiculous pin the tail on the reindeer game. Then I delivered her to her door safe and sound without bringing up her ex.

I did, however, send a text to Jeremy the next morning, feeling torn between my loyalty to Jeremy and to Remi.

> Thought you'd want to know, Mark cheated on Remi. That's why they broke up.

His answer was immediate, and I could hear his furious voice in my mind.

> WTF? Now he's going to get it.

> What are you going to do? Remi doesn't want him beat up.

> I won't touch him.

I glanced toward the ceiling of my work truck, then grabbed my hard hat to go on site for the inspection. Jeremy could do a hell of a lot without touching someone.

Although I'd been mostly dreading the party, I had to admit Remi wasn't the only one who'd had fun. She was a great dancer, kept me laughing, and when she'd hugged me on her porch after the party, I was shocked at how good she felt in my arms.

Blowing out a breath, I opened my truck door and forced my thoughts to the four high-rises I was in charge of. No time to think about beautiful women. Especially not when that woman was Remi. *Get a grip, man.*

The short week flew by. I spent Thanksgiving with Jeremy and Remi's family, not having any of my own relatives in town anymore. My parents had divorced and moved out of state my senior year of high school. Lucky for me, Jeremy's parents had offered to let me stay with them to finish out the year. After that, I'd worked construction and put myself through college at night. It became a tradition to spend the holidays with their family since mine were usually on a cruise or with their new spouses' families. One Thanksgiving with one of my stepfamilies was enough for me. The last couple of years that I was away, holidays had consisted of frozen pizza and a TV—quite a depressing difference from the warm, food-filled home with Remi's family.

Remi stayed busy Thanksgiving Day, either helping her mom, Nancy, and older brother, Chris—a chef—in the kitchen or playing outside with Gunner, who was determined to eat everything in sight. We spoke a little, keeping things superficial, which somehow felt odd now. Mostly, I watched football with Jeremy and his dad, Nate.

When we sat at the dinner table, decked out with a huge turkey and all the trimmings, I took my usual spot next to Jeremy, across from Remi. After grace, we started passing dishes around.

"So," Remi said, slightly louder than normal, "the strangest thing happened yesterday."

My shoulder muscles tightened of their own accord. I glanced at Jeremy who sat serenely at my side.

Remi scooped mashed potatoes and kept her tone level. "Mark found a dead skunk in his BMW at lunch." She passed the bowl along to her mom. "The stench was so bad they had to tow his car to the dealership to see if they can get the smell out."

My muscles ratcheted down another notch. *Oh shit.*

She paused as if in thought. "I wonder how a dead skunk could have crawled into his car."

Jeremy took a sip of water and shrugged. "Maybe it died after it got inside."

"Not unless it got run over by a car while inside it." Remi leveled a stare at Jeremy. "Why did you put a skunk in Mark's BMW?"

Chris barked out a laugh and tried to cover with a cough.

"What?" Jeremy played the innocent angel. That act had gotten him out of so much trouble in high school. "Why would you think I did it?"

"Because you put a dead skunk in Michael Derby's car sophomore year and one in Greg Shasta's car senior year," Remi said calmly. "Don't even try to play innocent with me. Just tell me why."

Nancy shook her head at the mention of Jeremy's wilder days, having been a frequent visitor to the principal's office throughout our younger years. And that was only for the things that Jeremy had been caught for. Nate rolled his eyes to the ceiling, but I got the feeling he wanted to pat Jeremy on the back and congratulate him in this situation.

The food suddenly didn't smell so tasty. She'd know I told Jeremy about the cheating, and I really didn't want to disappoint Remi by betraying her trust.

Shit, shit, shit.

"I don't care what you say about the breakup being mutual. He hurt you," Jeremy said, holding her gaze levelly. "I don't need any more reason than that."

She considered him for a minute while the rest of us held our breaths.

"Don't do anything else." She pointed her fork at Jeremy, then took a bite of potatoes. A smile played at her lips. "You should have seen his face. I thought he was going to cry." She let her head fall and her shoulders shook with laughter.

The table collectively relaxed.

"Well," Nancy said. "While I can't condone vandalism, I have to say I find this very fitting."

TWO DAYS LATER, ON SATURDAY, IT WAS MY TURN TO USE THE relationship ruse at a party. My company used the long weekend to throw their celebration downtown. I'd told Remi there was no reason to go, but she'd refused to miss the elegant spread at the downtown hotel. *Good practice to make a convincing couple*, she'd said.

This time I wore a suitcoat over my dress shirt but couldn't bring myself to choke with a tie on all night. I rang the doorbell and heard Gunner's barks as he barreled for the door to look out the narrow window at the side. Shaking my head, I considered the pup. He had a good heart, but as he grew, he was getting harder and harder for Remi to handle.

She didn't seem to have it in her to really take charge of him. Worry niggled the back of my mind.

That thought, and any others I might have had, evaporated the moment Remi opened the door. Her last dress had been a knockout, but this one made my jaw drop. It took a conscious effort to snap my mouth shut. The black material accentuated every curve, hugging her waist, then flaring out to stop mid-thigh.

I could only stare. Gunner's exuberant greeting broke me from my stupor. I tore my gaze away to give him a good pat, then held up a hand. "Sit."

He obeyed and waited, completely focused on me. "Heel." I held my hand above his nose, so he followed me at my side as I walked in the house. Remi had been working with him. I could tell because he knew the commands, but he wouldn't listen to her for more than a minute.

She shook her head. "I'm giving you a dog for Christmas."

I held back a smile. I'd love to have Gunner. He was smart as hell, had a pure heart, and would make a fabulous companion once he was out of the puppy stage. But I wasn't home enough to take care of him. "You'll get the hang of training him. Just be firm and strong."

Something in her expression made me pause. I'd said something wrong. I released Gunner and stepped in front of Remi, my mouth drying. "What's wrong? Did I upset you?"

"I'm good, just not feeling so strong right now." She shook her head and ducked away. "I'm really excited about a party at the Hotel Teatro."

I chewed on my lower lip but didn't push the issue. On the counter, I spotted a pile of expensive jewelry. "You need to move this before someone sees it through the window and breaks in."

Remi waved me off. "I'm going to throw it away."

"What?" I choked out. "At least sell it and use it for the—"

I cut myself off before I said house. "Therapy bills for the man hating syndrome he caused." I recovered.

She laughed. "I don't hate men." She paused, as if considering. "Well, I don't hate my brothers, or Dad...or you."

Seedlings of warmth sprouted in my chest, and I smiled.

We headed out after setting Gunner up in the kennel, not that he ever stayed in the thing for long.

The party was in one of Denver's most exclusive hotels—also owned by the development company that was building the high rises. White twinkle lights covered the main ballroom and tasteful gold Christmas decorations hung from the ceiling, casting a golden glow over the entire space. Casino tables filled one side of the room and a dance floor covered the other.

Remi slipped her arm in the crook of my elbow and squeezed. Walking in with her on my arm, I lifted my chin a little higher and confidence filled my stride.

A photographer held up a hand. "Let me get a photo of the gorgeous couple."

I would usually have waved him off, never a fan of pictures, but something made me stop instead. Remi leaned into me and I put my arm around her, smiling. The camera flashed and Remi leaned up—several inches taller in her heels—and kissed my cheek. The flash went off again.

"That was great," the photographer said. "These will all be available to download."

The warmth of her lips on my cheek lingered like a brand. "What was that kiss for?"

She lifted one shoulder. "Good practice. Our next party is the big one."

My gut fell several stories to the ground floor of the hotel. Sara's party. I'd forgotten.

Remi cupped my chin with her hands. "Hey. No going and getting all freaked out. We're going to have fun tonight."

She grabbed two drinks from a passing waiter and pressed one into my hand. "Tonight is only you and me."

I tossed back the drink, not even tasting it, as her words sank in. The alcohol warmed me as it traveled down.

"Wanna get lucky?" she whispered in my ear.

I nearly choked, my insides twisting like a pretzel. "What?"

She motioned to the casino tables. "Let's try our luck."

My organs resettled to their natural positions. "I've never been too lucky when it comes to gambling."

"I can't believe they give each of us five hundred bucks to play with. Most companies it's like Monopoly money." She pulled me to the tables and ordered our chips. "I'm thinking Blackjack, unless you want to get crazy and play roulette?"

"Blackjack sounds good." I let my hand rest on the small of her back, guiding her through the crowd to a table with two empty seats. A couple of my foremen were already at the table.

"Cade," one exclaimed as I took my seat. "Hey man, didn't think you were the type for company parties."

I inclined my head toward Remi who sat next to me. "She didn't give me a choice."

His gaze swayed to Remi. "I didn't realize Cade had a better half. Great to meet you."

"You as well," Remi replied.

I rested one arm on the back of her chair, an obvious signal to any guy around that she was with me. When she leaned into the crook of my shoulder, something clicked inside my chest. The protective feeling wasn't new to me, but the slight possessiveness knocked me back a bit. I didn't even have a right. Remi was just a friend...

I took two more drinks from a passing waitress. Remi's warmth ate through the layers of my jacket and shirt to seep into my skin. I leaned down and kissed the top of her head, inhaling her scent. She snuggled into me more.

"Twenty-one!" the dealer said.

Remi pulled away from me, both arms in the air. "You won!"

I hadn't even been paying attention to the game. Cold invaded where she'd been. I shook my head to clear my obviously muddled thoughts and high-fived her. We got into the game—Remi losing, me winning. I was up a thousand and had a crowd of people rooting me on. But Remi's excitement was all that really mattered.

Although I'd much rather have had her winning—especially with the financial problems Mark left her with—the cards kept coming my way. Maybe I could slip her my winnings. I certainly didn't need them with the sign-on bonus I got and living like a monk for the last three years.

An announcement came over the speakers. "In ten minutes, we're going to be wrapping up the gambling and dancing until after dinner."

Two thousand up, I cashed in my chips. Remi had a hundred left.

"Can we stop at the roulette table really quick?" she asked.

"Of course. And you can use my money after dinner," I said. "I don't mind."

She sent me a wink and walked to the roulette wheel as the dealer was calling for last bets. She put her hundred in chips on the twenty-two square.

"All bets in," the dealer called and rolled the ball in the spinning wheel.

I perched on a high barstool and watched the numbers fly by. The silver ball rattled through the slots, bouncing along. It settled in the twenty-two slot but teetered like it was going to roll out. I held my breath. The ball fell back.

"Black twenty-two," the dealer called. "We have a winner."

"Yes!" she exclaimed, jumping into the air. Her heel caught on the carpet, and she toppled sideways. Before I knew what had happened, I'd caught her and settled her in my lap. She inhaled sharply, her eyes meeting mine, her arms around my neck.

The urge to kiss her washed over me. And not some peck on the head or cheek. I wanted to claim her lips. I'd never wanted anything or anyone more in my entire life. She fit so perfectly in my grasp, so right.

It hit me like a sledgehammer right to the gut.

I loved spending time with Remi, and not just as a friend. I didn't know when it had happened. Maybe it was a slow change. But my heart warmed whenever she was close.

I was falling for Remi. Or I'd already fallen.

"Here are your winnings, miss," the dealer broke the moment before I could act on my urge to kiss her.

Remi straightened and pulled herself to her feet. "Thank you. Please cash me out."

She had won a thirty-five hundred dollar payout.

"Can you put this in your pocket?" She held out the thick envelope.

I nodded. *Makes it easier to put my twenty-five hundred in with yours.*

"This is the best Christmas party ever. Even without Santa," she said under her breath. Her gaze met mine. "You can't tell me this wasn't fun."

I couldn't speak to disagree with her even if I'd wanted to. All I could do was nod again and struggle with the revelation that had me thrilled and wanting to puke at the same time. My heart had been closed off for nearly three years. Leave it to me to fall for the one woman in the world that was off limits.

❄

WE DANCED, AS WE HAD BEFORE, BUT THIS TIME WHEN I HELD Remi in my arms, it was another feeling entirely. I cradled her, cherished her, and couldn't help but notice every touch of her body against mine.

"Oh," Remi said, out of breath, "I need a drink."

On a whim, I kissed her fingers. "I'll be right back."

There was a bit of a line at the bar. When I got back, she was talking to a guy I recognized as the marketing guru for the company. He and his team had half the units in the high-rises sold even before we broke ground.

I handed Remi the drink and settled my hand at the base of her spine.

"Hey." She grinned and waved to the man. "Cade, this is Mr. Macintosh."

I nodded. "We met at the preliminary meetings before the groundbreaking."

"I remember," Macintosh said. "I didn't realize you were dating this brilliant woman. Her campaign on Mile High Brewing was absolute genius."

Pink flooded Remi's cheeks, and she glanced down at her glass. "I'm surprised you knew about a relatively small campaign. And it was a team effort."

"You were the team lead," Macintosh insisted. "Take credit where credit is due. Besides, I make it my business to monitor all the up-and-coming talent in the marketing field. And you, my dear, have talent."

"She is definitely amazing," I agreed.

"Well," he pushed away from the high table, "you both have a great night, and I look forward to seeing you again in the future."

Remi sent me a wide-eyed stare as he walked away. "Holy crap. I can't believe he knew about my campaign."

"I can. You're incredible." I tapped her glass with mine.

CHAPTER 7

REMI

S<small>ARA'S PARTY HAD ARRIVED</small>. C<small>ADE, TENSE AND FIDGETY AS A</small> fifteen-year-old boy on his first date, stood next to me as we walked into the rented party space—a back room at an exclusive restaurant. I'd sprung for having my hair professionally done. And a new dress. The satin sheath slid over every curve of my body when I walked, in an almost sensuous movement. I needed to show up Sara. *For Cade, of course. Not for me. What do I have to prove?*

Forget that my confidence was at an all-time low. I was barely scraping by to cover up how weak and broken I was. Gunner could certainly see it. The dog didn't think he needed to listen to me. I guess Mark had done more of a number on me than I wanted to admit. But tonight was about Cade. I put extra flounce in my step and sparkle in my grin. *Fake it till you make it.*

Poinsettias covered every flat surface of the room, and mistletoe hung from the archways. Green and red ribbon spooled down tastefully from the ceiling in the shape of artistic Christmas trees. It was absolutely beautiful. But Sara always had impeccable taste.

"Cade!" an unnaturally high voice called.

We turned, and Sara held out her arms to him. Her slinky, metallic dress could have come off a runway in Paris and made me rethink wearing the Santa hat. Sara pulled Cade's stiff body into a hug.

Her empty ring finger attracted my gaze and alarm bells rang in my head. *Now that she knows what she missed out on, she might want him back.*

Her gaze fell on me, and she acted surprised, although she'd obviously seen me. I was hard to miss in the deep red dress and Santa hat. "And Rosie, was it?"

I kept the bite out of my voice. "Remi."

"Oh, right." She waved me off in an obvious slight and slung her arm through Cade's, putting herself between us.

Oh yeah, she wants him back.

Seeing her touch Cade sent two very separate emotions coursing through me. On one hand, they'd been together for years—it looked natural. But a larger part of me flooded with a bitter jealousy that surprised me. I bit the inside of my cheek. *This girl needs to be knocked down a notch, or ten. Is it rude to punch the hostess?*

Cade stopped, neatly stepping away from Sara and holding out his hand to me. "Come on, babe. Ready to party?"

I caught the shadow of a tremor in his voice and gripped his hand in both of mine, then squeezed. "Always, hon."

Sara shot me a veiled glare. In return, I sent her a saccharine grin that could have rotted teeth, and nestled in closer to Cade, my gaze on hers the entire time. *If looks could kill, I'd be dead.*

I didn't know what her game was, but no way was I letting her get her poisonous, money-hungry claws into Cade again. He needed someone who appreciated his sweet heart, loved his humor, enjoyed simply being with him. Someone…like me. *Wait, what?*

Cade must have noticed me stiffen under his arm. "You good?"

"Great." *Not freaking out at all.* "We got this," I said for both of us.

Sara stiffly showed us around, introducing Cade to some people and waving over friends he hadn't seen since before he left. It was about as comfortable as walking through a cave with vipers around the corners and enormous spiders ready to drop from the ceiling.

Cade kept me tight to his side, and I felt the tension in his frame. Though he may have some old friends here, they weren't good ones. No real friend of Cade's would have been cool with Sara after that shredding of a speech at the wedding. *Why did I insist we come?* I might as well have pushed him into Sara's grasp.

Sara finally released us to fend for ourselves when she needed to greet more arriving guests and we made for the food to keep busy. I had to admit, the Christmas gingerbread was to die for. I wished I could ask where she'd gotten them. *A fattening treat to bring in for Kerri…*

I excused myself to run to the bathroom and considered my reflection. The Santa hat was cute, especially with the bells on the end. But at this swanky party, I more needed an evening gown fit for the Oscars, not the simple dress I'd chosen. Blowing out a breath, I headed back out.

Sara was hanging on Cade's arm, laughing way too loud at something he'd said. That did it. A very un-holidaylike feeling bubbled in my chest. Now I really wanted to smack the smile right off her face. What the heck would it take for her to get the hint to leave Cade alone? He was taken—sort of. At least as far as she knew.

Then I spotted exactly what I needed a few feet behind

Cade. I strode over and didn't apologize for interrupting their conversation. Instead, I playfully pushed his chest to nudge him back.

"Oh, my," I said with a fake innocence. "Look what we're under."

He glanced up at the mistletoe hanging down on a bright red ribbon, then back down to me.

I sensed Sara's glare on my back, hot as laser beams. Wrapping my arms around his neck, I smiled playfully and whispered, "Time to put our acting to the test."

His widened eyes flashed with something as he hesitated for a split second before bending down to meet my lips. The warmth of his mouth spread over my entire body. Sparks danced behind my closed eyes, and jolts of electricity shocked me. I opened my mouth, and he deepened the kiss. No kiss had ever been so right. What started out as a play to prove something turned into one of the most epic moments of my life.

We broke away as hoots and claps filled the room. Scrambled fragments of thoughts tried to make it through my brain, but not much made it. *Cade... kissing... me... holy crap.*

I glimpsed Sara storming off. At least my plan to get her off his back had worked. But part of me wondered what in the world I'd started. Because it was definitely something.

CADE WALKED ME TO MY DOOR AFTER THE PARTY. I'D KEPT UP A semblance of coherent conversation on the ride home, despite our kiss running through my brain on repeat. We stopped on the porch, and I turned to him before I put the key in the lock. My senses seemed to have a new addition, as if my body recognized Cade and where he was, how far away, what he was doing.

"...before I leave?" Cade finished a sentence that I'd completely missed.

I don't want you to leave at all. The thought made me blink. Somewhere in all this pretending and acting like we were a couple, I'd really fallen for him. And not a guy-I-have-a-crush-on kind of way. More like the L-word kind of way. *Holy crap.*

My lips burned with the memory of his mouth against mine. I wanted—no, needed—to feel him again. Before I could psych myself out of it, I reached up and gripped the hair at the nape of his neck and tugged his head toward mine.

He stiffened for a moment before our gazes locked and he moved toward me. "Remi—" my name a whisper on the breeze. His hands settled on my hips as if they belonged there, and he pulled me against him as our lips met.

Same as before, sparks erupted behind my closed lids. Every nerve in my body jumped to attention. The sparks exploded into fireworks. His hands roamed over my back, and I explored his chest, arms, and neck. This connection wasn't only physical. A sense of safety like I'd never experienced before washed over me.

"Remi," he breathed as we came up for air. "Oh, God. Remi."

We dove back in for another kiss.

A bark right behind the door made us both jump. Cade broke the kiss and crushed me to his chest, ready to defend me in a way that made me want to laugh and cry simultaneously at how sweet he was.

"I'm going to strangle that puppy," I giggled.

Cade blinked and a completely unfamiliar expression took over his features—fear, with a dash of *oh shit*. He set me at arm's length. Away from his warmth that had surrounded me moments before.

Every cell in my body screamed at me not to ask, but I couldn't keep the question inside. "What's wrong?"

He shook his head. "I don't know what I was thinking. We can't do this, Remi."

My warm heart froze as if dipped into liquid nitrogen. "Do what?"

"This." He waved between the two of us. "Your brother is going to kill me."

I closed my eyes and gritted my teeth. Not the words a girl wants to hear after that kind of make-out session. "My brother has nothing to do with us. Don't use him as an excuse."

"And you're fresh out of a relationship," he continued. "I can't be your rebound guy. I have too much to lose."

My eyes snapped open. "Is that what you think this is? Me falling for the first guy I see to get over Mark?" Fury dropped my voice to a deadly calm. "Give me more credit than that. And who are you to say I'm on the rebound? Like you're over Sara?"

"I'm sorry," Cade said and stepped away as if more distance between us would stop the gravitational pull of our bodies towards each other. "I shouldn't have kissed you. I should never have agreed to this mess. I don't want to lose you as a friend."

The word *friend* stung like acid being poured over a fresh wound. I wanted to argue with him, convince him we had something real between us. But my pride dissolved those words to dust on my tongue. I wasn't pathetic enough to beg a guy to be with me. I fumbled with my keys to have an excuse to turn away.

Gunner peered out the side window next to the front door, his nose pressed to the glass.

"How did you get out again?" I asked the dog so I could ignore Cade. "I put a lock on the kennel."

"Need some help with him?" Cade asked.

He regretted kissing me, but he wanted to help with the dog. Fabulous.

"No, I'll be fine." Steel hardened my words. "You need to leave."

I unlocked the door and greeted Gunner, who lay at my feet and looked up at me with clouded eyes. His subdued behavior set off alarm bells. I considered him and crouched down to rub his ears. "Were you naughty?"

He whimpered. The alarm bells increased to full-blown sirens.

Against my wishes, Cade walked past us into the house. "Uh, Remi?" Cade called from the kitchen. "Come in here."

As I rounded the corner, my breath caught in my throat. The pile of jewelry that I'd left on the counter for weeks was now strewn across the floor.

I glanced at Gunner, who slumped against the doorway. My anger and hurt shot to the back burner. "He wouldn't have eaten it, would he?"

Cade's face scrunched and he shrugged. "I wouldn't put it past the little piranha. You need to go through it to see if anything's missing." His gaze assessed the passive pup. "He doesn't seem right."

"I can figure this out." I kept the upset from my voice by sheer power of will. "It's not your problem."

Cade caught my arm. "Remi, don't do that. I'm here for you." He stared at his feet. "And I care about Gunner."

"Good to know you care about one of us," I snapped, then wished I could grab the words out of the air and stuff them back in my mouth.

"I care," Cade said, his voice full of gravel and sorrow. "Too much, is the problem."

I shook him off. "I don't have time for this. I can't make

you leave." I moved to the strewn jewels. "Check him over while I see if anything is missing."

THREE HOURS AND A TRIP TO THE EMERGENCY VET LATER, Cade dropped me off at my house again. This time, I refused his offer to walk me to my door. It had been hard enough sitting in the waiting room with the tension between us thick enough to choke on.

"He'll be okay," Cade called before I closed the truck door. "He's a tough little snot."

I gripped Gunner's collar in my hands. They'd cut it off when the clip stuck. I nodded, then wiped another tear away and closed the truck door.

The x-ray showed Gunner had eaten two rings, including my engagement ring, an emerald pendant, thankfully without the chain, and two diamond bracelets. His digestive tract was practically a high-end jewelry store.

The vet held off on surgery to see what he could pass on his own. So, he was staying at the animal hospital for at least a day, possibly two. Plus, if he went into distress, they could get him into surgery immediately. I'd okayed whatever interventions needed to save him. All the chewed furniture, ripped pillows and other puppy annoyances seemed like nothing when I considered the possibility of losing Gunner.

Cade rolled down the window. "Remi, call and let me know how he's doing, please."

I nodded, not trusting my voice. Mad as Cade made me with wussing out on feelings I knew he had to be having, I appreciated that he genuinely cared about Gunner.

With the door locked behind me, I leaned against the wood. The already empty house now felt like a vacuum without Gunner's exuberant, chewy presence. *Why didn't I throw the damn jewelry away?* I slid down the door and rested my head on my bent knees, hugging Gunner's collar to my chest. What had started out as an amazing evening had turned into a nightmare that made me feel more alone than I'd been in my life.

"Mom," I pleaded. "I was fine at home."

My mom pulled me through the shop door on the main strip of old Castle Rock. "Nonsense. I heard it in your voice the minute you picked up the phone."

Note to self: never answer when Mom calls again.

"You don't need to be alone worrying about the puppy." She considered a rack of handmade scarves. "Besides, I know you're behind on your Christmas shopping."

If only she knew I had yet to buy a single present with two weeks until Christmas. She'd probably have an aneurism right there.

The enormous store was decked out in fake snow and holly. It was usually one of my favorite places to shop, filled with booths of local crafters and merchants. It was the best place to find one-of-a-kind gifts that you could feel good about buying.

Firming my shoulders, I breathed in the scent of hand-made candles, dried flowers, and beeswax. A chink in the chain of worry loosened. I wandered from stall to stall, picking up wooden carved kitchen utensils and jars of local honey or salsa. I bought Chris several types of hot sauce and found a hand-carved hockey plaque for my dad. Mom even coaxed a laugh out of me when she suggested we buy Jeremy a fuzzy alpaca hat.

"What are you going to get Cade?" Mom asked, her back to me.

I flinched at the sound of his name. Reality came crashing down with the weight of several tons. *What do you get the guy you fell for and then got rejected by in the same night? Laxative-laced chocolate? Icy Hot hemorrhoid cream?* "I'm not sure," I said, hearing the unease in my voice. I cleared my throat. I'd heard you could order a chocolate penis that was delivered anonymously. That idea had potential. "Something for his new place?"

Mom turned. "Something wrong between you two? I thought he was helping with Gunner."

Nothing gets by this woman. "Nothing's wrong," I lied—badly. "I'm upset over everything. With the dog, I mean."

An overly excited voice shriveled my eardrums on contact. "Remi?"

I spun to face Kerri and faked a smile while my insides turned to water. "Hey, Kerri. Good to see you." *God, I have to get Mom out of here. Fast.* "We were just leaving."

"Oh," Kerri beamed with a triumphant gleam in her eye that screamed, *I won.* Like she was so proud of herself for stealing Mark away from me. "I'm not sure where Mark got off to."

I closed my eyes and counted to ten, hoping this was a nightmare I'd wake up from. I opened them and saw pure fury on my mom's face.

Mom's gaze darted from my likely horrified expression to Kerri's obviously protruding belly. "We have time, honey," Mom practically purred. She turned her attention to Kerri. "You work with Remi, if I'm not mistaken?"

Kerri put on her sweet, innocent façade that had fooled me for all those months she'd been sleeping with my fiancé. But she was pushing it by talking to me in public. Maybe she thought we were all good because I didn't stab her with scissors at work…or throw staplers at her head…or smash her in the face—I cut off the violent train of thoughts. She obviously had no idea I was purposely bringing in sweets to make her fat. *Geez, I'm a horrible person.*

"We do." She rubbed circles on her belly absently, then leaned toward me, holding up a Christmas ornament. "I was thinking this would be perfect for Mark & I, for our tree. What do you think?"

The silver house was engraved with *Our First Christmas Together*.

I opened my mouth, but my tongue refused to make words.

Mom stepped closer and plucked the ornament from Kerri's hand. "This is for you and Mark?"

Kerri nodded, a flash of fear on her face that she quickly covered with her I'm-so-sweet expression. "We moved in together after... Well, I'm sure you know the entire story. I'm so grateful that Remi and I can still be friends."

Mom flashed a smile that only family would know as predatory. Her voice was serene. "Of course, Remi is an amazing woman." She examined the ornament. "This is perfect."

Kerri breathed an audible sigh of relief.

Mom turned away, then, as if reconsidering, returned her attention to Kerri, leaning in close. "In the spirit of forgiveness and friendship, it is Christmas, after all." She tilted her head toward Kerri's. "Just remember, many men start cheating when their partner is pregnant. And once a cheater, always a cheater." She straightened and took my limp arm, then beamed a smile like she'd wished them a long happy life together instead of the complete opposite. "Well, so nice to see you, Kerri."

Mom pulled me away from a gape-mouthed Kerri. Her firm grasp on my elbow was all that kept me from walking into the many tables crowding the space. She ranted under her breath. "I knew he cheated."

Tears pricked my eyes, but I blinked them away. "I'm sorry, Mom. I couldn't talk about it. Especially having to see them together every day."

Out of Kerri's line of sight, she pulled me to face her, cradled my cheeks in both her hands, and kissed my forehead. "You have nothing to apologize for." Emotion lowered her voice to a whisper. "My poor angel. To think you see that woman at work. How have you been holding yourself together?"

"I've been bringing in doughnuts and cookies," I managed to get past my closing throat.

Her brow furrowed, then understanding dawned. She barked out a laugh. "Serves her right. I hope they have to roll her into the delivery room like an Oompa Loompa."

I bit my lip but couldn't keep the giggle inside. Finally sharing my revenge with someone made it oh so much sweeter.

CHAPTER 8

CADE

I CHECKED MY PHONE FOR THE TENTH TIME IN AS MANY minutes. Still no word from Remi. She'd only answered one of my many texts, and that was with one word. *No.*

One foreman frowned, his attention on me instead of the pile of blueprints on the table in front of us. "You good, Cade?"

I clipped my phone to the case on my belt and nodded. "Yeah, my dog is at the vet. I mean, not mine..." I let my voice taper off. How do you explain your fake girlfriend, who is like a sister to you because she's your best friend's sister—except you might have accidentally fallen in love with her—and she has a dog that you're attached to as well, and he ate twenty grand worth of jewelry and might need major surgery? I shook my aching head. "It's complicated. When are the skylight panels arriving for installation?"

"Six weeks," another foreman answered.

I shook my head and forced my thoughts to the hundred different deliveries, trades, and workers that I organized and managed. "We won't be ready. Push the delivery back two weeks so the installers won't be waiting on us to finish the framing."

The rest of the status meeting went by, and I managed not to check my phone once. As we were wrapping up, it buzzed, and I snatched it from the clip like a kid with a present on Christmas morning—fast enough to earn several odd looks. The text wasn't from Remi. It was from my old high school buddy. My anticipation crumpled to dust.

> Hey man, we're looking forward to seeing you this weekend at the party. I wanted to give you a heads up that Sara somehow got wind and is coming. My wife didn't know about your past with her. I heard you have a new girlfriend, so I hope you're cool with that. See you Saturday.

Cement invaded my blood vessels and hardened. Sara was coming to the party. Why the hell? Nausea washed over me. For years, I'd thought I messed up the best relationship I'd ever have by not being good enough for someone like her. At the party last weekend, Sara had practically hunted me like a prized animal, pouncing every time Remi was more than a foot away. And instead of making me feel good, she made me want to run fast, in the opposite direction. The party had been hell.

Until the kiss with Remi under the mistletoe.

I hadn't let myself think about that kiss. It changed everything. All the emotions that I'd been blocking up inside had flooded out. I couldn't deny my feelings for Remi. Then, I'd been too weak to stop myself from kissing her again on her porch—she was lucky I hadn't done more. If Gunner hadn't interrupted us, I had no idea what would have happened.

I took off my hard hat and wiped sweat from my brow despite the freezing December temperatures. I'd messed this situation up so badly. If Jeremy got wind of me fake dating his sister, I might have been able to explain my way out of it, but now that we'd kissed? Well, I'd probably end up with more than a skunk in my truck.

I'd lose the only family that I really had left. My heart twisted painfully. I needed to explain to Remi why we couldn't risk being together. I'd happily take a beating from Jeremy. But I didn't know if I could take losing her parents and brothers if we broke up. Nancy was the one who'd convinced me to move back to Colorado. Nate's firm grip around my shoulders held me up at the altar when Sara shredded me and left me—my own dad being on vacation with his new wife's daughter and family.

I had to make her see. But to do that, I had to get her to talk to me.

Chewing on my inner lip, I typed out a text, then erased it four times and retyped before hitting send.

> The next party is Saturday night. What time should I pick you up?

My phone dinged as soon as I'd clipped it at my waist.

> You can go alone since no one important will be there, or not go at all. We both know that would be easier.

I sighed. Her anger came through loud and clear in the tone of her words. Plus, she was right. Usually, I'd skip the party altogether.

> Actually, Sara managed to get invited.

I hesitated before I texted the next part, gambling.

> I guess I can tell her we broke up? If that would make you more comfortable.

> What the hell? No way. Pick me up at eight.

I bit back a grin. Yep, Remi was still way competitive. A sour taste lingered in my mouth at having to use Sara to manipulate her, but I needed to get her talking to me.

> Is Gunner doing okay?

She sent back a reply.

> He's passed one bracelet and both rings, but they're worried about the second bracelet binding up his intestines.

There was a pause and the bubbles popped up that she was texting again.

> And I guess he figured out how to get out of the kennel, so they had to lock him in a room.

Worry tightened my grip on the phone even as a smile at his antics curved my lips.

> He'll be okay. He's a fighter.

She didn't respond.

I SPENT THE REST OF THE WEEK PLAYING OUT CONVERSATIONS in my head to convince Remi the myriad of reasons we couldn't be together but could still be friends. I wasn't sure I'd even convinced myself.

After two days of waiting, the vet had performed surgery on Gunner to remove the diamond bracelet. I'd gone to see him after work at the animal hospital. Even partially sedated, he'd tried to get up and lick my face.

The bill for the surgery and hospital stay was already over ten thousand—which the receptionist was willing to tell me since she'd seen me when we brought Gunner in. I'd left my credit card number and asked him to charge half the bill and mark it as a charity donation. No way would Remi accept my help if she knew, so I couldn't pay the entire amount.

I rang the bell at eight sharp. Remi yanked open the door, stepped out, and closed it behind her without even a hello.

"You look amazing," I said.

Her slanted glare was her only response.

Okay, not in the mood for compliments.

We drove across town in tense silence. I couldn't stand that our easy comradery had been destroyed. I ventured onto a hopefully safe topic. "I stopped in to see Gunner yesterday. He seems to be getting some spunk back."

She kept her gaze on the passing buildings. "He gets to come home hopefully by next Wednesday if his recovery goes well. I'm taking a few days off work to stay with him."

"Is that a good idea with the promotion up for grabs?" I asked.

"What choice do I have?" she snapped, but without heat. "Besides, Mark is probably going to get the position no matter what I do."

I hated the defeated tone in her voice. And I hated even more that I'd contributed to that. "Remi, you deserve the promotion more than that asshat."

"Can we not talk about it? We have this party to get through and then my work party, if you still want to come."

"Of course, I'm coming," I said. "I wouldn't leave you to face those two alone."

She grimaced, but nodded. "Thanks."

The party was in full holiday swing when we pulled up.

"Hey, see the Santa on the roof?" I pointed out the blow-up Santa in beach attire with a daiquiri in one hand and a beer bottle in the other. "And I've never seen Mrs. Claus looking so fine." Santa's wife sported a skimpy bikini that showed ample assets. Next to her, a blow-up of Rudolph smoking a cigar waved in the breeze.

"You hate Christmas decorations," she said with a sideways glance.

"Those are funny." I laughed, desperate to catch a glimpse of the Remi that I knew. "If not child-friendly."

At least her sigh wasn't filled with anger.

The front door was unlocked with a sign that said *Come on in to party!* We strode in and pine scent with a dash of alcohol blasted me in the face. This was going to be a rowdier party, by the looks of things. They set up an entire bar in the living room with a professional bartender twirling shakers of drinks before pouring out lines of shots.

No soothing Christmas music here. Loud rock played over the speakers. I took Remi's hand and couldn't miss how her body stiffened at my touch. She didn't lean into me as I led her through the crowd.

"You want to find something to eat?" I shouted over the noise. As I finished the sentence, I spotted my personal Grinch weaving her way through the partygoers like a snake in the grass. Sara's expression could only be described as predatory, and I couldn't help but feel like I was her prey of choice.

Remi saw her as well and leaned up to speak into my ear. "No food. I'm going to need a couple shots to get through this." She yanked me toward the bar with surprising strength for someone her size. "Two shots of whatever that is and a beer," she called to the bartender, waving at the pink shots he was pouring out, then turned to me. "You want anything?"

Oh, shit. I knew from past experience not to comment. "I'll stick with water since I'm driving."

She shrugged and threw back one shot, then the other, before taking her beer. "Okay, sweetie, let's get this over with." The way she said *sweetie* sounded more like an insult than an endearment. She wrapped her arm around my waist and leaned into me, obviously spotting Sara, who had redirected to follow us. "Oh goodie, here she comes."

The warmth her touch elicited was immediately doused by her words. Sara sidled up next to us at the bar. "Hey! Cade, I didn't know you'd be here."

Remi snorted and I jumped to speak before she could say something overly rude. "Yeah, there are a lot of my high school buddies here."

"Well, I love a good party." Sara beamed brighter than the north star. "But I don't know very many people here, if you wouldn't mind introducing me?"

Instead of cradling Remi under my arm, I was feeling like I'd captured a wild tiger cub that I needed to contain. *Maybe coming to this party was a mistake.*

At that moment, I realized my real mistake. Jeremy walked in the door. As if guided by fate, his gaze swept the room and settled directly on me—with Remi in my embrace.

His eyes widened, and a look that I couldn't read shifted his features.

Shit shit shit. I should have known Jeremy would be here. We had the same friends. But with everything going on with Remi and the dog...

"Cade?" Sara said, holding out a shot to me.

I shook my head, my gaze darting back to Jeremy as he made a beeline for us, and every macho bone in my body seemed to disappear. "Uh, no thanks."

"I'll take his," Remi piped up and grabbed the shot and

slammed it. The drinks, back-to-back, were going to hit her hard.

"Remi, slow down," I whispered.

Her glare screamed that I'd overstepped. I wanted to say more, but Jeremy approached us.

His tongue rolled over his teeth, and he crossed his arms as he considered Remi in my embrace. His tone was even, giving nothing away. "Hey, guys. Having fun?"

Sara gave me a playful shove in the arm. "This one is being a total bore. But it's great to see you, Jeremy."

Jeremy didn't spare her a glance. His attention was on me. He jerked his head to the side. "You want to talk?"

No, I'd rather jump in a tank of hungry sharks. "Sure, man."

I released Remi who leaned against the bar and ordered another beer. This night was going down fast. I followed Jeremy to a corner, my feet heavier with every step.

He turned and leaned against the wall in what most would assume was a relaxed pose, but I knew better. "I asked you to keep an eye on Remi. You taking that a little far?"

My brain sputtered with partial explanations, half sentences, nothing that made sense. "I... We were helping each other out with our exes. Just to get through the holidays."

His eyes slitted. "So, why is she over there guzzling shots like a freshman?"

I glanced back in time to see Remi clink glasses with Sara and take another shot.

"She's upset." I couldn't come up with any excuse, so the truth poured out of me like an avalanche. "I'm so sorry, man. I fell for her before I knew what was happening. I told her we can't be together because I can't lose your friendship, Jeremy, or your family. Plus, she's on the rebound." I paused to see his reaction. He stared at me like his face was made of granite. "I tried backing off and not hurting her, but I think I screwed up."

That got a snort out of him. He pushed away from the wall and leaned in close so no one around could hear. "Are you really that stupid?"

I flinched. "I swear we never…"

Jeremy held up a hand to stop me. "Do you actually think I'd be pissed at you for dating my sister?"

My tongue was frozen in confusion, so I nodded.

He huffed and put a hand on my shoulder. "I don't care if you fall for her. What better guy could I ask for to take care of my sister?" He pulled me in a little closer and his grip tightened. "But we have a serious problem if you break her heart."

I blinked. "I figured you'd hate me if you knew I loved her."

It was his turn to be surprised. His eyes widened. "You love her?"

It was the first time I'd even admitted my feelings to myself. I swallowed audibly as the truth sunk in. "Yeah, she's amazing."

"I don't need to hear the details. But sounds like you should probably tell her how you feel." He released me. "I don't want to have to deal with another skunk. I had to throw away my favorite pair of jeans after the last time."

I watched him walk away, too stunned to move. I'd never considered that Jeremy would actually be okay with Remi and me dating. *And you've already messed it up.*

A commotion returned my attention to the bar. Sara was getting in Remi's face, pointing her finger in a position that was way too familiar. I'd been on the receiving end of that anger way too many times. I rushed over.

"How dare you?" Sara exclaimed.

"What's going on?" I demanded.

Sara's furious glare melted off her face like snow in the Colorado sun. "Oh, thank goodness you're here." She stepped closer to me. "You won't believe the horrible things this…this girl has been saying."

Remi rolled her eyes in such an exaggerated gesture that I was surprised they stayed in her head. Her voice was slurred, the shots catching up with her. "Yep, I'm horrible."

Sara tried to snuggle under my arm. I stiffened and gently but firmly set her away from me. The shock on her face, wide eyed, mouth agape, gave her an expression that reminded me of a fish.

Sara sputtered. "Aren't you going to do something?" She waved a hand at Remi. "She said I was a lying snake, and ugly, and no one wanted me around."

"Didn't say that," Remi said.

Sara continued. "And that I was stupid."

"Kind of said that." Remi smiled.

Sara's glare could have melted the polar ice caps. "And that I should take my gold-digging expedition somewhere else."

Remi nodded once. "Definitely said that one."

Sara lifted her chin in victory. What I knew from experience to be fake tears glistened in her eyes. "You're going to let her treat me this way?"

She was so used to me following her every wish, jumping at her whim. For years I'd dedicated all my time to making her happy. I'd tried so hard, sacrificed anything and everything she asked.

Finally, I realized that our relationship had been doomed from the beginning. And not just because Sara was a narcissist, but also because I'd let her get away with it. Really, the biggest favor she'd ever done me was walking away on our wedding day.

Weight that I'd carried around with me for the last three

years fell away. I was finally over it. Relationships weren't supposed to be so hard. I considered Remi, who was watching me with increasingly teary eyes to see how I reacted.

"Cade," Sara almost shrieked. "Do something. How can you let her treat me this way?"

She must have been so sure that if she crooked a finger, I'd follow again.

I considered Sara and spoke in a soft voice, "How people treat you stopped being my responsibility a long time ago." I turned to Remi. "Hey, you want to get out of here?"

Remi nodded. "I think I might puke."

I bit back a grin and took her hand, leaving Sara staring after us.

With Jeremy's help I got Remi to my truck and buckled in. Jeremy waved as I pulled away from the curb and I didn't miss the smirk on his face. By the time I got her home, Remi was passed out in the front seat. I carried her inside and tucked her into bed. She mumbled and rolled over. I watched her sleep for a minute in the too quiet house, hating to leave her alone without even Gunner to keep her company, but knew staying wasn't a possibility. Then I smoothed her hair away from her face and knew that I could only hope that I hadn't already messed up beyond forgiveness.

CHAPTER 9

REMI

I WOKE WITH A BASS DRUM POUNDING IN MY TEMPLES. *WHY DID I drink so much?* I never did shots. For good reason. Glancing around, I realized I was alone, and relief and sadness fought in my heart. Cade got me home safely, like I'd known he would, or I'd never have let myself get drunk.

Jeremy showing up had been a shock, though I should have considered the possibility. The look on Cade's face flashed in my mind. Upset and fear.

Moving slowly, I stripped off the dress, brushed my teeth, downed ibuprofen, and got into the shower. The expression on his face wouldn't leave my mind. Here I'd brushed away his concerns over my family as excuses, but now I saw them for what they were. Reality.

I stood under the stream of water and remembered Jeremy leaning into Cade while they were talking, his face hard. I didn't care what my brother thought. If he was upset, he could get over it. But Cade obviously cared. They'd been friends since grade school.

I am so stupid.

I gingerly washed my hair.

Plus, my family was practically his adopted family. If we got together and broke up, what did I have to lose? A friend, which was a huge consideration. But Cade stood to lose my entire family.

I leaned against the tile. If I couldn't be with Cade, then I wanted—no, needed—to still be friends with him. My life was better with him in it. My breath solidified in my lungs at the thought of not being with Cade, of possibly seeing him fall in love with another woman.

Being by myself for a while is better anyway.

Focused on setting things right and feeling more like myself than I had in months, I got out of the shower. I'd missed two calls from the vet. Nausea threatened to overwhelm me. I dialed back. My frantic sentences bombarded the poor man that answered the phone.

"Sorry we scared you." The vet came on the line as I paced around my bedroom. "We were trying to get a hold of you to let you know that Gunner took a turn last night."

My heart stopped pumping. Darkness circled my vision.

"He's significantly improved and ready to be picked up if you have someone to stay with him for the next week," the vet finished.

I exhaled a stale breath. "Oh, thank you so much. I'll be right over."

Hair still wet, no makeup, and dressed in pajama pants and an old t-shirt, I looked like a college student the morning after a frat party. I ran into the vet's office and leaned on the front desk. "I'm here for Gunner."

"We have him ready for you. If you'll sign this statement." He handed over a piece of paper. "We already ran your card."

I didn't want to see the number but had to. *Damn, that's half what they told me to expect.* Never able to keep my mouth shut, I had to ask. "This is a lot less than we talked about."

"Your boyfriend paid for half of it when he came in," he explained.

"I suppose he didn't want you to tell me?"

The man cleared his throat, obviously sensing that he'd stepped in a mess. "Yes, but I can't really lie about payments."

I chewed on the inside of my cheek. *Really Cade?* It was such a classic Cade move that I couldn't find it in me to be mad. He'd never let me pay him back. *Looks like you're getting a six grand Christmas present.* "Thanks for letting me know."

Behind me a door opened, and another nurse walked Gunner out on a slip leash. He limped, so frail and weak. All thoughts and upset forgotten, I dropped to my knees and held out my arms. "Oh, baby." Tears spilled from my eyes. I'd been so afraid that my indecision over dealing with the jewelry had killed him. He scrambled into my embrace and licked my face. His warmth filled the space that had been so cold since we'd had to bring him in. "I missed you so much."

"He'll need to be kept calm. The meds should help some," the nurse said. "He's been getting more agitated, so that's why we thought he might do better at home. But you really need to keep the cone on him, so he doesn't lick."

I got Gunner to quit squirming, besides his whip-like tail. "I'll keep him mellow." I nuzzled his face. "And you're going to wear the cone of shame."

"He can't be left alone for at least a week. The stitches in his intestines can rip easily, even with something like jumping up. If that happens..." He didn't need to finish the sentence.

I met the nurse's gaze and spoke with confidence. "I won't let anything else happen to him."

I kept a hand on Gunner the entire drive home, as if to reassure myself that he was really there, alive. The house felt normal again with Gunner back. Well, nearly normal, since he needed to be kept lying down and the only way to do that was to lie with him. We cuddled all day Sunday, which my hangover was grateful for. While we were on the couch, I gave him a break from wearing the cone around his neck.

Monday and Tuesday, I called off work, not caring about my boss' tone. The promotion was at the bottom of my list of worries at this point. Wednesday and Thursday, my mom insisted on coming over so I could go into the office. She'd had dogs her entire life, plus raised kids, so I trusted her to watch over him, though I was sure she would be a softie when it came to him wearing the cone.

Friday, Cade showed up at my front door at seven thirty. I stared at him standing on my porch. "What are you doing here?"

"I'm here to take a Gunner shift." He strode past me into the house. Gunner was already running for him, the white plastic cone wobbling on his neck. Cade held up a hand. "Stay." Gunner stopped, but his head drooped. Cade approached and knelt in front of the pup, rubbing his ears slowly. "Hey big guy. You had us worried."

The emotion in Cade's voice stopped my protest. He really loved Gunner. I'd planned on staying home from work again, but today we had a huge presentation. "Are you sure you can miss work?"

"I haven't missed a day of work since I started this job." He rested his forehead against Gunner's. "He's so skinny."

I crouched next to them on the floor. "He's actually gained some weight, but he still needs to be resting."

"I'll take good care of him." Cade met my gaze. "Remi, I'm sorry."

I held up a hand. I hadn't planned on talking about this yet, but the sooner the better. "No. Don't be sorry. You were right."

He blinked. "I was?"

I got up and led Gunner to the half torn up couch that I'd

covered with sheets and made into his sick bed. "I'm the one who's sorry. I didn't consider how much you had to lose if we got together and then broke up."

He opened his mouth, but I pressed on. "My family is your family. I can't ask you to risk our friendship and all those relationships. I might not care about what my brothers think, but now I see why you do."

"Remi—"

"Let me get this out." I met his gaze and spoke with more strength than I'd had in a long time. "I want you in my life—even if that's just as friends. I was being selfish and stupid." I glanced out the window. "Besides, you're right. I'm totally on the rebound, all messed up. And that's unfair to you."

Words seemed to die on his lips. He nodded, then focused his attention on Gunner who practically vibrated with excitement. "Keeping him calm is going to be a full-time job."

Both relief and grief filled me, but at least I'd gotten out the words that took me a week to think up. The only part that I hadn't meant was the part about being on the rebound. I was so over Mark. But a girl had to save some face.

"I'm going to get ready for work. Thanks for this."

"What are friends for?" Cade asked, without looking at me.

My mom volunteered to stay with Gunner for the final part of the fake dating fiasco—my company party. I'd thought I'd want to spend hours making sure I looked great, but I threw on a simple knee-length sheath dress and plopped a Santa hat on my head instead of spending time on my hair. I truly didn't care what Mark thought.

Gunner sat in the doorway to the bathroom watching me, finally out of the cone of shame, since he wasn't licking at the incision. I finished my make-up in record time, keeping it simple. Gunner had been regaining his strength and feistiness as he healed but was still in danger of tearing his internal stitches.

My hairbrush fell to the floor and Gunner darted forward to pick it up and run away. It was his chase-me game.

Oh, crap.

Instead of running after him, I snapped. "Gunner, drop it."

He slid to a stop in my bedroom and let the brush fall from his mouth.

I stared. *He did it. He listened to me.*

Rushing over to pick up the brush before he changed his mind, I rubbed his favorite spot behind his ears and kept my voice level, though I wanted to fall to the floor and smother him with kisses. "Good drop. Yes, good drop. Come," I said. He followed. When I stopped, he stopped and sat next to my feet, like we'd practiced so many times on leash, but he'd never really listened before. I closed my eyes to keep tears back, then walked to the couch. "Sit."

His butt hit the floor and he watched me.

"Good sit. What a good boy." I couldn't keep some enthusiasm from my voice and his tail wagged. *I can do this. See, I am strong.*

The doorbell rang.

Now for the big test. I got up. "Stay."

He whimpered but stayed put as I went to the door.

Mom and Cade stood on the step. I paused at seeing the two of them together—Cade with a slightly sheepish expression on his face. My mom, on the other hand, looked like she'd won some sort of prize. I shot Cade a furrowed brow, but he just shrugged. *I can't deal with this right now.*

"You're beautiful, honey," Mom said. "Where is my baby?"

She'd fallen for Gunner's sweet personality in the two days she'd taken care of him.

"Gunner, come," I called.

He scrambled to the entryway and leaned against Mom to get love.

"That's my baby," Mom crooned. "I brought special treats. Yes, Grandma loves you."

Cade shot me a mirthful grin that my mom caught.

"What?" she demanded. "They had special healthy Christmas cookie treats at the pet store." She waved us out the door. "You go on. I've got a nice evening planned for Gunner and me."

I grabbed my purse and closed the door.

"I wonder what she's going to be like with grandkids," Cade laughed.

Emotion thickened my throat as I longed to take his hand in mine, but held back. "She'll be waiting a while."

THE PARTY WAS ABOUT AS PATHETIC AS YOU COULD GET. A tinsel tree straight from the seventies stood in one corner along with a dud in a Santa suit that I had to wonder if my boss picked up from the front of a liquor store. Cold cuts with sliced bread graced the food table, along with a store-bought cookie tray and a cheap shrimp ring. With the record profits that I knew we'd brought in, you'd think they could throw a decent party. At least there was alcohol. But after last weekend, I wasn't up for drinking.

"Who was in charge of putting the party together?" Cade asked.

I nodded toward where my boss stood talking to a younger man I'd never seen before. "I saw the budget. He had plenty to spend."

Cade shook his head. "Must have given himself an extra Christmas bonus instead. You holding up okay?"

"I'm good. Great. Fabulous." Nerves made the food even less appealing.

Cade held my hand—for show—but I enjoyed the feel of his skin on mine anyway. Too much.

Mark and Kerri avoided us. Guess Kerri hadn't gotten over Mom's comments at the shops. So sad. Not.

Pretty much everyone ignored the pathetic food and went for the hard alcohol. Within an hour, everyone except Kerri, Cade and I were drunk. Several women even sat on creepy-Santa's lap for pictures.

I leaned in to whisper in Cade's ear. "As soon as they announce who got the promotion we can get out of here."

"You sure?" Cade asked. "That room temperature cheese is looking pretty tasty."

"Right?" I quipped. "But I'm really waiting for the shrimp to go bad because what's better than food poisoning over Christmas?"

Our banter, so easy and natural, lessened some of the agony hiding in my heart. *See, being friends is good.* But my heart stamped *return to sender* on that memo and refused to stop aching.

"You okay if I head to the bathroom?" Cade asked.

"I'll try to restrain myself from the urge to sit on Santa's lap."

"Don't you dare do that without me," Cade said. "I want photographic evidence."

With a shake of my head, I shoved him toward the bathroom. He'd barely been gone a minute when Mark appeared at my side.

I jumped and tried to back away, but hit the wall beside me. "Hey, Mark."

He smelled like he'd showered in tequila rather than drinking it. "You look good, Remi."

I glanced around for Kerri, hoping she'd come over to claim her drunk man. He wasn't my problem anymore.

Mark leaned in. "She went to lie down. Man, is she getting fat." He moved closer. "I miss you."

I turned to stare at the asshole I'd thought for three years was the man of my dreams. To think I'd cried even a single tear over him. "You are such a pig." I smacked away his raised hand before it could touch my cheek. "Don't even think about touching me."

"Is there a problem?" Cade's voice, deep and heavy with threat, came from behind us.

I neatly side-stepped Mark and stood beside Cade. "No. No problem worth our time." I led Cade away, which, given his stiff stature, was no easy feat. "No beating him up. You promised."

"He deserves a lot worse than a skunk," Cade spat.

"They had to total his BMW," I whispered.

"That means he gets a new one." Cade wrapped his arm around me and glared across the room at Mark.

Before I could respond, my boss stepped to the center of the room. "If I could have everyone's attention."

Ice crystals formed in my blood and circulated, freezing my extremities. This was it.

"We had a record year, thanks in a large part to all the hard work out of this office," he continued.

And that's how you're moving up to the main office in New York.

"I know there's been a lot of speculation about the future now that I'm leaving." Tense silence filled the room, and I could feel eyes on me. "I don't want to keep you in suspense." He waved to a man standing over in the corner that I'd noticed earlier and assumed was someone's guest. "This is my son, Frankie. He's a year out of getting his master's and will take over for me."

Stunned silence filled the room, followed by a wave of whispers and a few weak claps.

I snapped my gaping mouth shut. I spoke under my breath, "A newbie? You've got to be kidding."

Cade leaned in. "Nepotism at its finest."

"Is this a joke?" Mark called from the other side of the room.

Our boss held up his hand to Mark. "I know you'll all welcome Frankie and show him the ropes."

Mark glowered and I was surprised smoke wasn't coming out of his ears.

Instead of anger, relief filled me. I needed this job for the money, especially with Mark breathing down my neck over the house. But before I could think, I walked to the center of the room with Frankie and his dad.

"Congratulations." I held out my hand and shook Frankie's. "I'm sure you'll do great."

My boss beamed at me with approval.

I turned to the gathering of people I'd worked with for the last three years. "I have an announcement as well." I met many of their gazes. "As of the new year, I'm leaving the firm."

A gasp spread over group.

I continued. "Since I already put in for vacation, my last day was yesterday." I held up my glass of sparkling cider. "Happy holidays, everyone."

Ignoring the calls and especially my boss' voice behind me, I walked to Cade. Peace filled me. "Ready to go?"

His scrunched brow smoothed when our eyes met. "Sure you don't want a shrimp for the road?"

We left the party, and knowing that I never had to go into that office again was the best Christmas gift I could have given myself.

Cade dropped me off. Mom left. I sat on the couch with

Gunner, alone with my decision to quit my job with no backup plan, no idea of what I was going to do or how I was going to pay my bills, much less buy Mark out of the house. But I knew I'd made the right decision. Thinking about not having to see Mark and Kerri again made me feel like my blood had been infused with helium. I was lighter. So light I might float away.

I snuggled Gunner who let out a contented sigh with his head resting on my chest. "We'll find a place with a nice yard for you, I promise." I stroked his smooth fur. "We've got this." I pulled my laptop to my side and got to work on my future.

CHAPTER 10

CADE

THERE WERE THREE DAYS BETWEEN REMI'S BOMB OF A HOLIDAY party and Christmas. I spent most of that time picking up the phone to dial her number, then stopping myself. She'd let me off the hook, said everything I should have been happy to hear. Except that I let fear get in my way—and a stupid fear at that, since Jeremy was cool as long as I didn't break her heart.

I'd been ready to tell her on Friday—until she'd said the word rebound. That changed everything. What if she didn't feel the same way about me? Doubt swirled in my head until I was dizzy.

Last minute Christmas shopping left me with one gift to buy—for Remi. I stared into the front display of a jewelry shop. Diamonds, sapphires, emeralds and sparkles like glittering lights were nearly enough to blind me. This was what Sara would have wanted—what Mark had bought Remi.

I moved on, walking until another shop window caught my eye. Finally, I knew what I had to do and stepped through the door.

❄

As I walked through the door to Nate and Nancy's house, the smell of breakfast casserole, cinnamon rolls, and spiced cider mixed to make a scent that was distinctly Christmas in my memories. It was the same every year and joy pushed out a bit of the anxiety filling my mind.

"Merry Christmas," I called as I closed the front door behind me. Gunner bounded to me, his recovery well underway. "Hey, big man." I set a stack of wrapped packages to one side of the tree. Gunner nosed the boxes, sniffing in earnest. "Leave it."

He huffed one more time, but obeyed.

I found everyone in the kitchen, gathered around the island where steaming dishes were cooling on the countertop. Chris pulled the strata, his spectacular breakfast specialty, out of the oven. How I'd dreamed about that casserole.

"Chris, I hope you made two of those. I could eat one all by myself," I said as my mouth watered in anticipation.

He laughed. "I'll be sure to send you home with leftovers."

Jeremy clapped my shoulder and handed me a glass of cider. "You made it."

I sipped the cider and tried to keep my attention off Remi as she rushed around to help set the table.

Jeremy's gaze assessed me, but I refused to flinch.

After a beat, he nodded. "Glad you're here this year."

"Me too."

I waited, returning Remi's wave when she came back into the kitchen but keeping up the conversation with Jeremy and their parents. She was doing an Oscar-worthy job of acting like nothing had changed, like we were old friends and nothing more.

What if it isn't an act? What if I really was her rebound? The rebound guy was easy to get over.

The twenty minutes it took to finish the table and get the food out seemed to take years. Anticipation increased to nervous jitters, which amplified to near full-blown terror.

The heavenly strata might as well have been sand for all I tasted it, but I put on what I hoped passed for a normal expression. Remi handed me the plate of cinnamon rolls and our fingers touched. Her gaze met mine and held.

My mouth went dry. Was it only my hope or was there more than friendship behind her eyes?

She blinked and let go of the plate.

I busied myself with taking an icing-covered bun and made a production of taking a bite, then wiping my mouth.

"I took your advice and pawned the jewelry," Remi said with a grin. "Well, all except the engagement ring."

I frowned. The word *rebound* ricocheting around my head like a dodge ball fired from a cannon. Trying to keep my voice level, I asked, "Why would you keep that piece?"

"Turns out cubic zirconia isn't worth much, even at two-point-five carats." She shook her head.

"Wait," Chris cut in. "He got you a fake for your engagement ring?"

Remi nodded while the rest of the table stared. "The gold setting is the only part that is worth anything." She didn't seem upset. She seemed solid, not that she'd ever been fragile, but now something had changed. Gunner lifted his nose to the table's edge and sniffed at the bacon on her plate. "Gunner, down." Her voice was strong. He obeyed without a thought. "Good down."

"He's listening to you," I said. "When did that start?"

"Saturday." She patted his head. "I don't know why, but it just clicked."

I knew why. It was written all over her, in the lift of her chin, the tone of her voice, the strength of her laugh. She was

Remi again. Not the broken version Mark had left. But the real Remi.

My smile hurt my cheeks. "He knows you're the boss."

She sent me a wink that warmed my entire body.

There's still hope for us. There has to be.

"Good thing you got some money from the jewelry," Nate said. "Since you quit your job without having another one lined up."

"Stop," Nancy shushed him. "My girl will always land on her feet."

Nate grumbled something about responsible adults but kept the rest of his thoughts to himself.

As tradition dictated, presents were next after we cleaned up breakfast. I couldn't wait any longer. I stood up after everyone had gathered in the living room. Gunner sat next to Remi. All eyes settled on me. Clearing my throat, I fought to remember the eloquent speech I'd rehearsed. Nothing. "I need to say something." *Wow, that was deep.* "I hope that you'll all humor me."

"Everything okay, Cade?" Nate asked.

I nodded. "Yes, sir."

Nate shot a look to Nancy, then both Remi's parents eyed me. "Must be serious," Nate said and waved between Jeremy, Chris, and me. "You haven't called me sir since you three totaled my Mustang doing doughnuts."

Jeremy settled back on the couch and got comfy like he was about to watch his favorite sitcom. I ignored his smirk.

"I…" Words failing me, I grabbed a flat box and handed it to Remi. "This is for you."

Her gaze was wary, unsure, but she ripped the paper and opened the box while her parents and brothers watched. She lifted out the embroidered dog collar with *Gunner* across the back. "Wow, it's great," she said and held it up to her neck. "Is it my look? I think maybe leather and studs would be better."

Heat rushed to my face. "There's more inside."

She dug around in the box. Gunner helped by tugging tissue paper out and mouthing it. Remi pulled out a small black velvet box. Her wide eyes shot to me while Nancy grabbed Nate's hand. Remi tilted her head to the side.

"I told you we couldn't be together. But the truth is, I was scared." I wondered where all the air in the room had gone because I was about to pass out. I rushed on. "I used Jeremy as an excuse, and your family."

"Cade—"

"No," I cut her off. "I have to say this before I pass out. I love you, Remi. I hope that I'm not your rebound guy. Because I fell in love with you, every beautiful, funny, genius part of you. I don't even know when. But I had to say this for everyone to hear because I hurt you, and I swear to all of you that if Remi gives me a second chance, I'll never hurt her again." I motioned for her to open the box.

She tilted the lid and closed her eyes, then opened them and took out a silver dog tag engraved with *Gunner* on the front. With a hand covering her mouth, she turned the disk over and read both our names and numbers on the back. Shaking her head, she set the box aside and got to her feet.

I couldn't breathe. She rushed to my arms and flung herself where she belonged—with me.

"I love you, too," she gasped, then kissed me full on the lips for all to see.

"Oh, gross," Jeremy protested. "We're going to have to set some ground rules."

"I knew it!" Nancy exclaimed and smacked Nate on the arm. "I told you."

Remi pulled away and looked into my eyes. "I have a confession. You were never my rebound. You're my everything."

EPILOGUE

REMI

THE STACK OF MOVING BOXES TEETERED, THREATENING TO fall over. I adjusted the top box and grabbed another to unfold and tape. Gunner ran past me with something shiny in his mouth.

"Gunner, drop it," Cade called from behind him.

The pup stopped and gently set the band of metal on the hardwood floor. I recognized the six thousand dollar watch that I'd bought Cade for Christmas to pay him back for Gunner's surgery.

Cade strode into the room and snatched the watch, clipping it to his wrist. "Can't turn my back on you for a second." He scolded the dog.

I handed Gunner the monkey he'd gotten for Christmas, and he bounded away. Box assembled, I wrapped a photo frame in paper and put it on the bottom.

"Are you trying to kill someone?" Cade eyed my stack of boxes. "We have plenty of floor space to make more than one stack."

"It's a challenge." I laughed. "Got to make it fun."

Gunner galloped by again, doing laps in the house. In two

weeks, he'd made a full recovery. The only way anyone would know that he'd nearly died and had surgery was his short, trimmed belly hair—and the still healing pink scar.

Cade leaned in to steal a kiss. I pulled him closer to get more of him. My phone buzzed in my pocket, breaking us apart with Cade mumbling something about timing.

Biting my bottom lip, I glanced at the screen—an email notification. The smile dropped from my lips.

"Hey, you okay?" Cade frowned. "Is it Mark again? I swear I'll do a lot worse than a skunk—"

I held up a shaking hand to stop him and opened the email. Scanning to the good part, I gasped and nearly dropped to the floor on weak knees.

Cade caught me. "Remi, talk to me, babe."

"I got it," I whispered, and held the phone out for him to read.

His mouth gaped when he got to the job offer and he dropped the phone to pick me up and swing me in a circle. "I knew you would!"

I clung to him and laughed. The resumes I'd sent out the night I quit had gotten some attention. I'd had two other job offers in the last week, but I'd been holding out hope for the one I really wanted. Mr. Macintosh had come through. And not with just any offer.

Gunner dropped his toy to prance around us, joining in the merriment without a care as to the reason. He bounded in a circle at our feet.

"Did you see that signing bonus?" Cade asked after thoroughly kissing me. "It's amazing."

"I know." I sucked in a breath, my head spinning.

Cade sobered. "You know..." he began, then paused.

His tone dampened some of my joy. "What is it?"

"Well, you could buy Mark out of the house with a bonus that size," he said. "You wouldn't have to move."

I tilted my head back and considered the high ceilings, the vast windows, the layout that had once been my dream, then returned my gaze to Cade's face. "I was actually thinking about something else."

His brows pulled together. "Oh no. Thinking is dangerous."

My expression grew serious. "I was thinking that I don't want to be in a house I bought with Mark." I forced myself to keep my gaze locked on Cade. "I was thinking it might be nice to find a place with you."

He blinked. "You…really?"

My heart stuttered as I freaked out over pushing him too hard, too fast.

"Remi, that's amazing," he exclaimed. "I wanted to suggest the same thing."

"You don't think it's too fast?" I asked.

He smoothed my hair back and cradled my cheek in his palm. "Too fast? I've known you for twenty years. If we kept up this pace, I won't marry you until I'm nearly eighty."

He leaned down to kiss me until a persistent wet nose and wiggling body pushed between us. "Besides," Cade continued. "We kind of already have a kid together, so not much of a leap to move in."

I barked out a laugh and pulled him to the floor so Gunner could get some snuggles. The pup leaned into me, his tongue lolling out in a huge doggy grin. This was family. This was love.

PLEASE REVIEW

We hope you've enjoyed *The Holiday Rebound* by Emily Bybee. Please take a moment to rate and review the book, as every review helps our authors. Thank you.

Rate and Review: The Holiday Rebound

MEET THE AUTHOR

Emily grew up loving to escape to the fantasy world of books. She began writing at the age of twelve after having a series of extremely vivid dreams that begged to be made onto a story. In high school and college she focused on science and graduated with a degree in environmental biology. After college she began writing again, but quickly realized she had failed to take a single writing or grammar class. Luckily, she's a quick learner. She now enjoys making up stories in multiple genres from urban fantasy to contemporary romance and loves to throw some science in whenever she gets the chance.

OTHER TITLES FROM 5 PRINCE PUBLISHING

Liz's Road Trip *Bernadette Marie*
Back to the 80s *S.E. Reichert & Kerrie Flanagan*
Granting Katelyn *S.E. Reichert*
Ghosts of Alda *Russell Archey*
The Serpent and the Firefly *Courtney Davis*
Raising Elle *S.E. Reichert*
Rom Com Movie Club No.3 *Bernadette Marie*
Rom Com Movie Club No.2 *Bernadette Marie*
Rom Com Movie Club No.1 *Bernadette Marie*
A Crossbow Christmas *Ann Swann*
Hot For Teacher *Felicia Carparelli*
The Happily Ever After Bookstore *Bernadette Marie*
Perfect Mrs Claus *Barbara Matteson*
Princess of Prias *Courtney Davis*
Paige and the Reluctant Artist *Darci Garcia*
A Spider in the Garden *Courtney Davis*
Megan's Choice *Darci Garcia*
Something New *Bernadette Marie*
Something Forbidden *Bernadette Marie*
Something Found *Bernadette Marie*